CVC
7

CVC

Carter V. Cooper

SHORT FICTION ANTHOLOGY SERIES

BOOK SEVEN

SELECTED BY AND WITH A PREFACE BY

Gloria Vanderbilt

EXILE
editions

Carter V. Cooper Short Fiction Anthology Series, Book Seven.
Issued in print and electronic formats.

ISSN 2371-3968 (Print)
ISSN 2371-3976 (Online)

ISBN 978-1-55096-725-8 (paperback). ISBN 978-1-55096-726-5 (epub).
ISBN 978-1-55096-727-2 (kindle). ISBN 978-1-55096-728-9 (pdf).

Short stories, Canadian (English). Canadian fiction (English) 21st century.
Vanderbilt, Gloria, 1924-, editor.
Series: Carter V. Cooper short fiction anthology series, book 7.

Text Design and Composition by Mishi Uroboros
Typeset in Garamond, Mona Lisa and Trajan fonts at Moons of Jupiter Studios

Published by Exile Editions Limited ~ www.ExileEditions.com
144483 Southgate Road 14 - GD, Holstein, Ontario, N0G 2A0
Printed and Bound in Canada in 2017, by Marquis

We gratefully acknowledge, for their support toward our publishing activities,
the Canada Council for the Arts, the Government of Canada,
the Ontario Arts Council, and the Ontario Media Development Corporation.

Canadian sales: The Canadian Manda Group, 664 Annette Street,
Toronto ON M6S 2C8 www.mandagroup.com 416 516 0911

North American and international distribution, and U.S. sales:
Independent Publishers Group, 814 North Franklin Street,
Chicago IL 60610 www.ipgbook.com toll free: 1 800 888 4741

In memory of

Carter V. Cooper

The Winners for Year Seven

Best Story by an Emerging Writer

∾ $10,000 ∾

Halli Villegas

Best Story by a Writer at Any Point of Career

∾ $5,000 ∾

Seán Virgo

CVC

Book Seven

PREFACE

I founded the Carter V. Cooper short fiction competition in memory of my son, and to champion literature, which he had loved.

It is one of the great joys of parenthood to behold, in astonishment and surprise, the depth and complexity of your children as they emerge into themselves. In that spirit, I cannot help but admire the writers who comprise *Book Seven* of the *Carter V. Cooper Short Fiction Anthology Series.*

Open to all Canadian writers, this annual short fiction competition awards two prizes: $10,000 for the best story by an emerging writer, and $5,000 for the best story by an established writer.

Believing, as I have said before, that all writing is born of a singular yearning to see a truth with one's own eyes, these eleven stories – in genre, range, tone, and interest – are all utterly their own.

About the winners: "Road Kill" – by emerging writer Halli Villegas – is a story completely in control of how it is for a person to crack up and fall apart, the kind of story that is very difficult to sustain, and sustain it Villegas does. Seán Virgo's "Sweetie" is an intelligent, witty story (again, the writer is completely in control of the material), that not only captures the pathos inherent in the brittleness of smart set conversation, but slyly, deftly, engages the darkness at the heart of that pathos. It must be added: that verbal brittleness – often pistol-whipping in its glibness – is more often than not, funny.

I would also like to give a big thank you to the readers who adjudicated this competition: the judge in charge, storyteller Matt Shaw, magazine and books editor Jerry Tutunjian, and poet and literary editor Dani Spinosa – as well as Mary Rykov who worked with several of the authors in preparing their stories for publication – all of whom have played their own special roles in the development and support of emerging writers.

Gloria Vanderbilt
September 2017

Halli Villegas

ROAD KILL

Her daughter squatted, studying something on the front step. Leslie saw Margery's blonde head, hair so blonde it was almost white, tilted in the position she took only when deeply absorbed. They would be late if they didn't get going now. They would be late and Leslie hated driving in the dark, especially on unfamiliar roads, roads that would take them farther and farther from the life they had into one that they did not yet know.

"Margery," she yelled, wanting to hustle the little girl along but knowing that it usually took more than one call. "Margery, come on."

Her daughter glanced up but did not move. From where Leslie stood beside the car she saw the ice-blue eyes, just like her ex-husband's, briefly light on her, measuring, wondering how serious mama was. With a small shake of her head, Margery went back to studying whatever was on the stoop.

Leslie walked over to the steps. Her daughter's thin shoulder blades poked through the sun-faded pink t-shirt like a bird's fragile wings, shifting slightly when she breathed. Reaching out, Leslie touched the girl's shining hair. "Margery, we have to leave now."

"Look, mama." Margery gestured with one hand, a curiously graceful gesture. Then she pulled back her arm and hugged her knee again, the blades of her back tense and still now.

On the front step lay a dead robin. Its eyelid at half-mast, head thrown back at a wild angle, yellow beak slightly open. It appeared as though in the throes of some ecstasy or other. This is what had caught her daughter's interest.

"Leave it, Margery. It's dead."

Margery uncurled her hand and put out a tentative finger to touch it. "No mama, it's not dead. It's just dreaming."

Leslie yanked Margery's arm. "Don't touch. Birds are crawling with bugs. It's dirty."

Margery stared at her mother, eyes wide. A blink, and then she stood up and took a step back, wiping her hands on her shorts. "But it's not dead. I don't want it to be dead. It's just sleeping."

Leslie took Margery's hand and said, "Come on, let's get in the car."

Margery followed obediently, but she looked back at the bird on the stoop. She saw the feathers riffle softly, once, twice. She knew the bird would wake up when they left, wake up and fly into the trees where it would watch their car pull away with Margery and mama.

In the car Margery sat quietly, resting her head on the window. The past two days of sorting through her toys, folding sundresses and sweaters, helping mama put everything in the boxes carefully marked Margery, had worn her out. Her head swayed with the motion of the car, dipping lower and lower, thumb creeping into her mouth. This was a regression. At six, Margery was too old to be sucking her thumb for comfort, but Leslie let it go. If she was honest, she wanted to do some self-comforting too. Not suck her thumb, but a nice bottle of Gamay Noir in a dark room would be good, would help a lot. She watched the yellow clapboard of the Cape Cod style house becoming smaller and smaller in her rear-view mirror.

That house had been Joe's idea; in fact, Margery had been Joe's idea. This shameful secret still caused Leslie intense guilt. At forty the idea of children, if that particular desire had ever been there, was long gone. She loved their life in the city. Theatre and museums, other childless couples over for drinks and dinner, long Sundays in bed with newspapers and bagels. It was the way she thought adult life was meant to be, *her* adult life. Joe wanted children. Joe wanted a son to throw a ball to, wanted the big clapboard house with the echoing rooms and the scurrying animals in the walls, and the slow drip of the faucet that could never be turned off or fixed properly and drove Leslie crazy when she lay awake at night listening. That was *Joe's* idea of adult life.

In the end, Joe left. Not for another woman. That would have been too predictable. He left because he was bored. He said that to her one night after dinner. "I'm bored. I want to have a life somewhere else, do something else."

He made this pronouncement at the oak trestle table he had picked out from Pottery Barn two years ago to match the sideboard and rustic light fixtures he had chosen from Restoration Hardware. Stunned, she sat there for at least an hour after he left the dining room, wondering what the hell just happened. Somewhere in the wall behind her an animal began to scratch, ceaselessly chewing at the insulation, the wiring, the wood. Leslie got up and in a fury banged her fist against the wall until the soft edge of her hand was numb, and the animal fell silent. It took a week for her fingers to stop aching and the bruise to fade.

Joe moved out, filed for divorce and took a sabbatical from his teaching post at the university. He went to Mexico and left her with the house she didn't want. They hadn't heard from him since, except a postcard to Margery, her name misspelled, showing a photo of a sugar skull from The Day of the Dead. Leslie sincerely hoped he ended up decapitated at the hands of a drug cartel. But since the alimony and support cheques were still deposited regularly into her account, she doubted that had happened. She could dream, couldn't she?

In the back seat Margery slept, her mouth slightly open and her head thrown back. She could be dead too and Leslie wouldn't know it. She might think Margery was just sleeping, but her little girl could be dead.

Leslie gripped the steering wheel tighter; she glanced in the rearview mirror. Margery slumped in the same position. *Oh God, what if she's dead, what will I do? I never wanted her. It's my fault.*

Leslie stood at the side of the road screaming. Motorists stopped along the shoulder, spraying gravel, their white faces staring at the crazy woman. Margery's limp body lifted from the car by a good Samaritan while she clung to her child's hand, trying to will her back. *I didn't mean it, please give her back.* Leslie jerked the wheel of the car to jostle some life into Margery, she had to know, *please give her back.*

In the rearview mirror Leslie saw Margery open her eyes, stare blindly for a minute and then shift position, settling her thumb in her mouth again.

Thank God, thank God. The road ahead stuttered through Leslie's grateful tears.

They stopped for lunch in a small town off the highway. Leslie woke Margery up, pushing the sweat-curled hair off her little round brow, marveling for a minute at the perfection of the lashes and lip line.

"No, I want to sleep." Margery protested.

When Leslie lifted her out of the back seat, Margery purposely made her limbs heavy and limp. Leslie set her down. She was too heavy to carry for long. Margery shuffled her feet on the asphalt of the parking lot. "Where are we? When are we going home?"

"We're having lunch, Margery, here in this nice restaurant."

With a fierce smear of her hand Margery pushed her curls off her forehead. They stood up wet and jagged. The new pin feathers of an unlovely chick.

"I don't want lunch here, I want to go home."

Margery twisted away when Leslie tried to take her arm. "It smells funny. Don't touch my arm."

A woman in matching green capris and shirt was getting out of her car. A small frown appeared on her face as she watched Leslie and Margery. Even from a quick glance Leslie recognized her as one of those women who think they have a way with children, especially other people's children. Smiling briefly in the woman's direction, Leslie carefully put a hand on Margery's shoulder. That woman was in denial. Children were unpredictable. With one touch her daughter might have a meltdown or snuggle lovingly into her side. A child's response had nothing to do with you and everything to do with them.

Margery screamed and stomped her foot, pushing her mother's hand. Leslie fought the urge to smack her.

"Come on, Margery. Maybe they will have ice cream." She marched ahead, not caring now about the woman. She held the door open for Margery. *Please God make her come, let her just come in the damn café.* Margery ran to where her mother waited and took her hand. Leslie knew she was not forgiven, yet, but was just the better part of a bad deal.

The café tried to look homey, with dusty ruffled curtains and a parade of wooden geese wearing blue kerchiefs on the wall, but the woman behind the counter had a milky eye. A fat bluebottle fly sat on an oozing piece of cherry pie under a scratched plastic dome.

Mother and daughter sat across from each other in a tufted vinyl booth. The seats were sticky, but Leslie didn't have the energy to wipe them off with a napkin. One had a little tear in the cushion and Margery stuck her finger in it, wiggling the tear open even wider. Leslie took a menu from the metal holder on the table.

Pulling a piece of grimy fluff from the hole in the seat, Margery asked, "Where's Daddy?"

"Mexico."

Margery tossed the fluff to the floor under the table and worried at the tear again without looking up at her mother.

"I want him to come home. Now."

"Well that's not going to happen." Leslie opened her menu. "Please stop pulling at that, Margery." Margery pulled her hand away and inspected her palm as if she were reading her future.

"Do you want a grilled cheese?" Leslie asked, trying to sound normal, like an adult.

Margery made a fist and glared up at her mother. "I want to see Daddy."

"Margery, Daddy is far away. He will be home soon, and then I am sure he will come to see you." *Pot pie, fish and chips, meat loaf.* Leslie read the smeary typing on the plastic page of the menu over and over to herself. *Apple pie, just like Mother used to make.*

"How is he going to know where we are if we aren't at home? I want to go home." Margery started to cry loud sucking sobs that made her gasp and choke.

Leslie put her head down on the cool surface of the Formica table. She smelled sour rag and ketchup. If she could just go to sleep now and wake up later, much later.

"Can I take your order?"

Leslie raised her head. The woman with the milky eye stood, pen in hand, at the table. The waitress smiled at Margery.

"Don't cry, sweetie. Why don't I get you a nice milkshake?"

Margery looked up at the woman and started to shriek. After tears, red-faced embarrassment, a fiercely whispered lecture on behaviour, an uneaten grilled cheese sandwich, and a half-eaten patty melt, they were back in the car again, pulling away from the little town and onto the highway. Margery stared out the window sullenly.

"The bird wasn't dead mama. I don't want it to be dead. It was sleeping," said Margery in a soft voice from the back seat.

"What did you say?" Leslie didn't turn her head. She was still back at the café explaining to the waitress and the woman about the divorce, about the trip, about how tired they both were.

Margery's voice, sharp with excitement, broke through her reverie. "Look, mama, that raccoon's sleeping by the road." She sat upright in her seat, pressing her face against the window's glass.

Earlier while Margery slept, Leslie saw roadkill all along the highway. She found it darkly humorous to pass signs that said Beaver Kill, Deer Kill as she drove past dead animals in various stages of decay. Black with rot or so fresh their fur rippled in the wake of the car, all of them were surrounded by birds, plucking at the broken bodies.

Margery's hand patted at her shoulder. "Can we stop and play with the raccoon?"

"Margery, it's like the bird. It's gone to heaven."

"It's asleep," Margery's voice rose. "I want you to stop."

"We can't stop."

"Look there's another bird, a big bird." Margery twisted in her seat to see out the back window. "Mama, it's going to fly away. I want to stop and watch."

Leslie looked at the side mirror and saw a dead crow on the shoulder. The bird was smashed almost flat to the ground with one wing sticking up. Leslie sighed. Margery could keep this up for hours. Asking to stop, asking for the animals to play, asking for her mother to make it happen. Leslie's head hurt, vibrating on the verge of tears. Maybe this was hell.

In a voice stripped of its motherly lilt she said, "Margery, it's dead. It's gone to heaven where it will see lots of other birds and be happy. Now sit back in your seat."

Surprisingly Margery sat back. It was quiet for a few more miles, and then Leslie heard Margery's voice again, low and thoughtful.

"Mama, do you want Daddy to be dead?"

Leslie looked into the rearview mirror. Margery met her eyes.

"Of course not, Margery, never. I would never want your father to be dead."

Margery didn't say anything for a moment, but she didn't take her eyes off Leslie.

"Mama, do you want me to be dead? Do you dream I'm dead?"

Leslie pulled the car over to the shoulder. She switched it off and turned in her seat. She reached around and put a hand on her daughter's knee. She could feel the bone there, hard and round, like a stone beneath the soft skin.

"Margery, don't ever say anything like that. I love you, sweetie." She stroked her little girl's knee with trembling fingers. "I'm just tired. And that's why I'm a little cross. When we get there, we can go to the zoo one day and see all the animals playing. Would you like that?"

Margery looked out the window into the trees that lined the highway, "I dreamed you were dead, when I was sleeping."

The light was fading fast, and they still had a few hours to go. For the past two hours, Margery hadn't spoken to her again, but Leslie caught her whispers every once in a while. "There's a squirrel I want it to be sleeping, there's a dog I want it to be sleeping, there's a cat I want it to be awake now."

Leslie switched on the radio to try to cover the sibilant demands coming from the back seat, but the stations this far out were spotty and faded in and out like voices heard through heating vents in old houses. Margery's litany went on.

The hypnotic roll of the tires on the highway, the dark stands of trees along this stretch, the sinking sun all lulled Leslie into a kind of rhythm. *Almost there, almost there.* It was full dark now, and the headlights illuminated such a small circle ahead that Leslie started to forget there was anything else but this road and her daughter's chant. She felt the little fingers clutch at her shoulder and heard Margery's whisper in her ear.

"Mama, what is that? Is it a dog?"

Alert, Leslie looked through the windshield into the circle of light her headlights cast. Half in the road, half beside it, was a dead deer. Impossibly slender, long legs trailed into the left lane of the highway, but the deer's body and head were settled on the shoulder. The animal's throat split open as if it gaped in one last cry.

Leslie drove around the deer, swerving into the other lane and back again. Her hands clutched and released over and over on the steering wheel. "Not a dog, sweetie, it's a deer. It's a deer and it's dead."

Margery pinched her shoulder, "Stop. Now."

"Sit back in your seat." Leslie tried to keep her voice calm.

"It's not dead, you liar. I don't want it to be dead. I want it to be here." Margery's hands were over her ears, and she shook her head back and forth, "I want, I want, I want, I want."

"The deer can't come back. It's gone, Margery." Leslie tried to make herself heard over the child's high-pitched wail.

"I want, I want. Liar, liar."

Her voice filled the car. Leslie could barely focus on the road, knew she would have to pull over. Desperate to stop the girl's screaming she scanned the roadside for a turnoff, a rest area. There were no signs, no scenic views, no picnic tables. Not even a goddamn weighing station. In the black emptiness of her rearview mirror, Leslie saw a shadow detach itself from the roadside behind their car. Its head at an angle, its legs splayed but still loping towards them.

"I want, I want, I want," Margery chanted over and over. She began to bang on the glass of the car window in rhythm with her words

Something that must have once been a bird dragged itself against the windshield, leaving streaks that made it impossible to see. Leslie stopped the car in the middle of the highway. The deer caught up to them now and began to rock the car, gently at first, and then more violently. One blind eye stared into the car window on the driver's side as its smashed face came closer.

"I want, I want, I want."

Everything dead along the road before and behind them began to rise and walk toward the car. Possums, crows, dogs, deer. Animals so mangled she had no idea what they were crept out of the dark.

Leslie heard the metal of the roof popping under scrabbling hoofs. The windshield cracked; the star of the impact spread and she could no longer see what was in front of her.

"I want, I want, I want." Red with effort, Margery's face loomed in the rearview mirror, her eyes wide and empty.

"Shut up, just shut up, shut up." Leslie started the car, but the tires slipped and spun on the remains of the swarming creatures. They would spiral off the road and into a tree, into a ditch. She couldn't drive away. Where was everyone, *where was everyone?* Leslie jerked to a stop and hit the horn, trying to scare the road-kill away from the car. She screamed too, as if her words would have any meaning. Still they came, streaming from the bush at both sides of the road, from the ditches and empty fields.

"I told you mama, I told you." Margery clapped her hands and started to unbuckle her seat belt, scrabbling at the clasp, pulling at the nylon strap.

Animals snuffled the edges of the windows, testing the strength with beaks and claws. The crushed and mangled snouts and beaks jostling for position were all Leslie could see.

Margery freed herself from the seatbelt. The frantic sound of her attempts to press down the door handle sounded like the lever of a slot machine being pulled again and again and again.

Leslie closed her eyes. A bottle of wine in a darkened room, the slow drip of a faucet whose rusted washer flaked away in the dark damp beneath the sink. She would never open her eyes, she promised herself. This time she would dream something else, dream them all dead and buried for good. Margery's door opened and it brought her back to the rocking car. Her daughter. Gone now, slipped from the car. Leslie pulled at her own door lock, popping it open. The seatbelt cut across her rib cage when she tried to get out. She fumbled with it, fingers numb and trembling, and just by chance pushed the release. Her foot caught and she almost fell, but she reached out and grabbed the door frame She steadied herself, pulled herself up, and looked for her daughter.

Outside the car the night was clear and silent. Haloed by headlights only for a short distance, the road ahead, empty. Nothing alive. As she stood still, waiting, she heard the faraway cry of an animal. From this distance, she couldn't tell if it was the despair of an animal caught in a trap or one running free, hunting for something it saw in the dark.

Iryn Tushabe

A SEPARATION

On the evening before I leave for university in Canada, I sit on the terrace of my childhood home watching Kaaka, my grandmother, make lemongrass tea. She pounds cubes of sugarcane with a weathered pestle. She empties the pulp into a large pot and tops it up with rainwater from a jerry can the same olive-green as her A-shaped tunic.

I step down from my bamboo chair and stride over to her. I lift the heavy pot and set it on a charcoal stove smouldering with red-hot embers.

"*Webare kahara kangye*," Kaaka thanks me in singsong Rukiga, the language of our birth. She comes from a generation of Bakiga who sing to people instead of talking because words, unlike music, can get lost.

I smile and sit back down in my creaky bamboo chair to read a copy of National Geographic that a British photographer sent me. His photograph of a troop of gorillas in my father's wildlife sanctuary is on the cover of the magazine, and the accompanying article quotes me blaming the Ugandan government for refusing to support our conservation efforts.

"I hope I don't get in trouble for this," I say.

Kaaka laughs the sound of tumbling water. "You flatter yourself if you think the fierce leaders of our republic have time to read foreign magazines."

She chops fresh lemongrass leaves on a tree stump, sniffing the bits in her hands before tossing them into the pan. The simmering infusion is already turning the light yellow colour of honey and will taste just as sweet. As the herb steeps, a citrusy fragrance curls into the evening like an offering. Kaaka fans the steam toward her nose and inhales noisily, closing her eyes to savour the aroma.

"The tea's ready," she says a short while later, rolling out a mat woven from dried palm fronds. She sits on it, legs outstretched, hands clasped in her lap. This is how it has always been with us. Kaaka makes the tea. I serve it.

I pull the sleeves of my oversized sweater over my fingers and lift the pan off the stove. With a ladle, I fill two mugs. I give Kaaka hers and sit down next to her, blowing on my cup before sucking hot tea into my mouth. Its sweetness has an edge.

"You'll do very well in your studies overseas." There is finality in her voice. When the invitation from the University of Regina's Anthropology and Archaeology Department arrived months ago, I showed her saying I would go only if I had her blessing. "You'll acquire some new knowledge and a whole world of wisdom."

"I'll be home for Christmas," I tell her now.

"Yes, you will. Something to look forward to."

Three weeks later, I'm standing by my open living room window looking down at the street, watching people go about the business of living. I arrived in Regina, Saskatchewan, on the tail end of summer. The August heat has turned my apartment into a sweltering cavern. Mr. Stevenson, the silver-haired professor who met me at the airport, will be supervising my doctoral research. He also found this Munroe Place apartment for me. I can't seem to say the street name right, though. Is it Monroe as in Marilyn Monroe, the deceased American actress? Or moon-row like a row of moons?

Two teenage girls walk by sharing a blue slushy. The one with a thick mass of coffee-coloured hair takes a sip and hands the cup over to her friend, whose short hair is tinted the bright pink of a well-fed flamingo. Sticking out blue tongues at each other, they double over in laughter. They're wearing high-waisted shorts so short that when they bend, I glimpse the lobes of their flat-flat buttocks.

Dark clouds have gathered above the high-rise across the street as though getting ready to pounce. But the sunlight pierces their serrated margins, turning them into silver beacons.

The sound of my cellphone jolts me. The call has a Ugandan country code.

"Kaaka!" I shout into the phone. My elation keeps her name in my mouth longer, making it last.

"Harriet, it's me," my father answers, his voice loud and strident. A call from Father frightens me a little. Always, I phone him. It's never the other way around. His preferred medium of communication is email – lengthy reports with headings and subheadings. The last one had an index and a couple of footnotes about his observations of infanticide amongst chimpanzees in Kibale Forest, our sanctuary's rainforest home. Did I know that contrary to previous observations of infanticide, deadly aggression in chimpanzees is not a gender-specific trait?

"Are you there, Harriet?"

I brace myself. "I'm here."

"It's about your Kaaka." Father's voice suddenly acquires an uncharacteristic softness. "She has died."

He likes directness, my father. And sharp things. He has a prized collection of spears and *pangas* in his office that he says our forefathers carried with them when they migrated from Rwanda many centuries ago. In this moment, his words are a machete that cuts me to the core. I feel empty as though the part of me that's most substantial has left, leaving me hollow. Only skin and bone.

My hand goes limp and slowly falls from my ear until finally the phone hits the carpeted floor. I can still hear Father, but his

A Separation

voice is now muffled and distant, reaching me as though through a tunnel. I lower myself into the dining chair that has found a permanent place by my living room window. I finger the cowrie shell necklace around my neck, wishing to go back in time before having this knowledge, back in time when I felt whole.

Time passes and it doesn't. Father's faraway voice through the phone stops, and silence eclipses the room. How long have I been sitting here, lost? He'll be worried, want to know I can be strong.

I hear the ping of email arriving. It's from Father. Kaaka went missing the evening before and when she didn't return by nightfall, he put together a search party. A game ranger found her body lying among the moss under a tree canopy behind the waterfalls.

"It was lucky he found the body when he did, before some wild animals got to it. That would have been gruesome," Father's email says. I wonder about the moment my Kaaka became *the body*. Did it hurt? Or was it peaceful?

Outside, the dark clouds have huddled closer together, blocking out the sun. Then slanted lashes of rain beat down from the sky, battering my windowpane like they want into the apartment.

I pull on my sneakers and fly down the stairs, a caged bird let loose. I run toward Wascana Lake, a path shown to me by Mr. Stevenson. Gaining speed, I part grey sheets of rain as hot tears run down my cheeks. Every few minutes, bolts of lightning fire up the black skies followed by a ripping sound like a great big cloth being torn down the seam. I splash through silver puddles pooling on the concrete lip of the lake. I want so badly to go back home.

"I'll have more tea," Kaaka says on the evening before I leave for Canada. But when I refill her cup, she sets it on the tree stump behind her, next to the Kerosene lantern radiating amber light into the dusk. She fishes a lilac satin bag from the deep pocket of her tunic and presses it into the palm of my hand.

27

"Hold onto these for me, will you?"

The bag's contents clink together as I loosen the string tie to reveal cowries, their porcelain surfaces gleaming like sea-polished rocks. Kaaka stretches herself out on the mat, looking up into the stars as though she hasn't just offered me an everlasting memory. This ninety-year-old woman who raised me would have given me the shells on the night of my wedding to wish upon my marriage the strength of the Indian Ocean. Except I haven't brought a suitor home, and at 30 years old, I've turned into an old maid.

"Have you also given up on me ever getting married, Kaaka?"

"Not at all," she says, still looking up into the indigo sky dotted with millions of stars, her hands forming a pillow underneath her cloud of grey hair. "I know you will get married. This is just my way of telling you that your worth isn't tied to marriage and procreation."

I try to undo the knot in the necklace I wear, the one I inherited from Mother after she died, but it won't loosen. It seems to have become tighter as the years have gone by. I keep tugging and pulling until eventually it loosens and comes apart. Mother had only six cowries on her necklace. Adding my new six makes it fuller, heavier. I'll be an old maid with twelve cowries around my neck, which is rare.

The light from the lantern makes shadows of the wrinkles in Kaaka's mahogany face. Lying there on the mat, she looks solemn as if trying to untangle knots from an old memory. I'm struck by how tiny she is, how little space she takes up on our mat. She reminds me of a stub of a pencil worn with its work, the best of its years shaved away.

My mother was a dressmaker. In my head, I have an image of her sitting behind her sewing machine on the front porch of our cabin, a yellow pencil sticking out from behind her ear. As the pencils shrunk, she'd shove them into her puffy hair. I always imagined the tiny pencils getting lost in that thick hair, getting trapped in its tangles, no way out. I wanted to save them but Mother never let me touch her hair.

"I can't remember her face," I say, lying down besides Kaaka. "Mother's face. The contours of it have faded." The realization, saying it out loud, hurts my chest. What kind of a daughter forgets her mother's face?

"You're the spitting image of her," Kaaka says. "Look into a mirror anytime and hers is the face that looks back at you. You have her voice, too. Sometimes I hear you speak and I think, Holy Stars! My daughter lives inside my granddaughter."

I was eight years old when Mother succumbed to the poison of a black mamba. That's when Kaaka came to live with Father and me. (Grandfather had left her years before to go live with a much younger woman.) On the day of my mother's funeral, Kaaka told me that Nyabingi, the rain goddess our tribe worships, had called Mother into the spirit world. She wanted me to understand that my mother still lived on, only now her physical presence was lost to us. I didn't tell her that her explanation was cruel, that it only made it harder for me to grieve for my mother.

"Tell me again how she died," I say, willing myself to accept her view of death, that it births one into a form of oneself bigger than life and visible only to the living whose eyes have grown eyes.

"You know how it happened. If you still have to ask, it means you doubt."

I'm a primatologist. I believe in verifiable, quantifiable data and logical explanations of the world. I was born in a cabin on the edge of a river and I see connections everywhere. I bridge between species, places, and time. I was six years old when I first learned the names of all the birds in our sanctuary, from the little Bronze Mannikin to the imposing Shoebill. I wrote them down in a notebook and recited them to tourists from Europe and North America like a morning prayer. I was ten when a baby chimpanzee hooted and purred his way into my heart. When we found him,

Father and me, he still clung to his dead mother's leg. A poacher had shot her and left her for dead. It was then that I decided to study non-human primates, to try and protect them from humans.

"But how do you know for certain that Nyabingi took her? How do you know if Nyabingi exists?" I hear myself ask Kaaka.

"Because her spirit has visited me every night since she passed on. That's how I know."

This is brand new information. I don't know how to respond to it so I lie there quietly, too many questions hanging in the air above me.

The day after Mother's funeral, Kaaka packed a picnic. She sat me down by the river and said, "Repeat after me: my mother has been ushered into the spirit world."

I repeated the phrase because she'd told me to, not because I believed it.

"Say it with conviction," She pleaded. "I'm certain of it the way I know that the moon is the moon and the sun is the sun."

I wanted to believe her. Really, I did. But when the customary week of mourning ended and I returned to school, I told anyone who asked that a snake which moves faster than most people can run, whose venom is so potent and fast-acting that only two drops of it paralyzes its victims, killing them within an hour, which has a head the shape of a coffin and a mouth blacker than the chimney of a kerosene lantern, struck my mother twice. Trying to get away from this snake, she fell into the nameless river that runs through the sanctuary, and the river spat her out at its frothy mouth where it feeds the swamp. That's more or less what Father had told me. The rest I had read in his big book on snakes of East Africa.

"Our dead are always with us," Kaaka is saying now. There's a hint of suppressed anger in her voice. "You must always remember this."

"I know but—"

"Why is it impossible for you to believe in a world whose existence you can't explain?" Kaaka speaks over my objection. "You are smart enough to know that just because you can't see something that doesn't mean it's not there."

A sort of electric hush charged with the loud singing of crickets sits between us. In the distance it creates, I probe the walls of Kaaka's theory of death, walls that are warped and distorted and never hold up whenever subjected to reason. But I suppose gods don't listen to reason. I suppose gods go about doing whatever they want even if it means leaving a trail of orphaned children and childless mothers.

"She just materializes at the foot of my bed like an image from a projector," Kaaka says. It takes me a moment to realize she's talking about Mother's spirit. "Except it's obviously not just an image because she tidies up in my room. She walks around picking my tunics from the floor and folding them and putting them away in my wardrobe."

"No!"

"She talks to me, too. It's a kind of wordless communication like the hum of the forest. It took me a while to understand it, but now I do."

I want to ask her what else Mother has told her, but I don't. If she wants to, she will tell me unbidden. And after a moment's silence she does. Kaaka wants me to know that mother's spirit has promised to escort her over to the other side soon, very soon. She wants me to be prepared for this possibility. I'm not to worry, though, she warns. I'm not to cry. This is the ending she desires. It's what she's always hoped for. I should want it for her.

"Will you come back and visit me?" I say, all of my sensible questions having deserted me. "When Mother takes you, will you come back to me?"

"If you want me to."

I don't know how long I've been running when a dog's bark stops me short in a dimly lit back alley. He's a large black dog with a rumpled coat like the skin of an elephant. A white picket fence overrun with vines separates us. He scratches at it with his paws before giving up and turning away from me.

The rain has let up, but I'm still dripping wet, cold to the bone. I resume running to generate warmth. A bearded man with a long whip of braided hair down his back is standing outside a convenience store. He yells his sexual desires at me in an alcohol-induced drawl. I run. When we are scared, time slows. I'm running so fast it feels as if I'm standing still and everything around me is a blur. It seems incredible to me now that an hour or so ago I thought staying in my apartment one second longer might kill me. And now that I've strayed too far and don't know how to get back, I want, more than anything, the safety of its concrete walls.

I see a street sign up ahead, Cameron Street. The houses on it look alike, old and eccentric. I run up to the closest one and ring the bell by its purple door. My heart is beating sorely against my ribs. My throat is burning.

"I'm lost," I tell the middle-aged woman who opens the door. Waves of chocolate-coloured hair frame her long face. "May I use your phone to call a cab?"

"Come in, come in," she says, pulling the door wide open. Then looking up a narrow staircase, she shouts, "Ganapati!" Her accent is East-Indian. Her body emanates warmth and the sweet smell of jasmine. She offers me a large towel from a linen closet.

A man comes down the creaking stairs wearing a frown on his face. His white slacks are folded up at the bottom like someone at the beach who wants to wade into the water without getting their clothes wet. When he sees me, he tilts his head at a questioning angle.

"Weren't you about to leave?" the woman asks him but doesn't wait for his answer. "Can you drive this young woman to her home so she won't be swindled by a cab driver? Their fees are exorbitant, aren't they?"

I nod my head yes, even though I've never taken a cab.

The man introduces himself. He says I can call him Ganesh.

I put his name on my tongue, toss it around my mouth, and push it out between my teeth. I once knew a man with the same name. Ganesh. He stayed in one of our guest cabins at the sanctuary for three months. He wrote poems in jagged cursive all day long. In between bouts of writing, he walked around on calloused feet, touching Kaaka's honeysuckles, cutting his fingers on her roses, sucking up the little beads of blood. In the evenings, he sat cross-legged outside the cabin and recited his day's work. Kaaka and I listened to him in blissful incomprehension.

I shake Ganesh's hand, and a symphony surges through my brain. His face glows as though he's lit from within. My body is in love with him, this stranger named for a god. It bends toward him like a vining plant to light.

"I love your necklace," he says.

"Thank you. The cowrie shells are a gift from my grand-mother Harriet. I'm named for her. My name is Harriet."

"A beautiful name."

Ganesh opens the passenger door of his blue sedan for me. He turns a corner onto 13th Avenue, and soon we are cruising down Albert Street. The shimmering surface of Wascana Lake is lit with fiery shades of gold and red. Where did I lose my way along this lake? Can we outrun fate?

"Here we are," he says, pulling up in front of my apartment building. "I'll walk you to the door."

I want to tell him that he needn't. That contrary to prevailing evidence, I'm quite normal. That running too far and getting lost was really the universe's doing, not mine. But I hear how alien this self-defense sounds in my head, how lacking in logic, and I let him walk me to the entrance of my building.

We stand at the door and I awkwardly fumble around my wet pants, feeling for which one of its many pockets hides the key. Finding it, I hold it up victoriously, evidence that I'm not crazy, not completely. But mad people probably think that they are the normal ones – everyone else is insane and should get help.

"I better get going then," he says. But he doesn't leave. We stand at the door as though held together by something outside of ourselves.

"Would you like to come in?" I ask.

"Sure. But I can't stay long."

Inside my apartment, Ganesh offers me the details of his life like a present. He left India five years ago to attend a music residency at the Regina Conservatory of Performing Arts, and then he decided to stay afterwards. Now he's a pianist with the local symphony orchestra. The woman is his aunt. She owns an Indian restaurant downtown, and he dines with her every Sunday. Would I like him to make us some tea? What kind of tea do I have?

"Lemongrass. I have dry lemongrass." I pull open a kitchen cabinet to find it. "I brought it from home in Ziploc bags. In cut-up bits. An airport security officer wanted to toss them into a garbage can."

"Why?" Ganesh says, his hazel-green eyes wide with surprise.

"He was worried I might try and plant 'whatever this stuff is' on Canadian soil."

Ganesh's laughter is the warm colour of hope. I excuse myself to change out of my wet clothes. When I return to the kitchen, Ganesh is tossing a fistful of lemongrass into a pan with water. As the lemongrass boils, its fragrance fills my apartment with the sweet smell of home. I close my eyes and inhale its aroma, remembering a time so recent yet so irretrievably gone.

Ganesh takes a sip of the tea and purses his lips; the taste hasn't lived up to his expectations. He sets the cup down on the kitchen counter and scribbles his phone number in my day planner that I left open after breakfast.

"You'll call me?" he asks.

"I will."

"You promise?" His high-pitched voice sounds like pleading.

"I do."

On the morning I leave for Canada, Kaaka puts her hand on my back and leaves it there as she accompanies me to my father's beat up Range Rover, caked with mud. We stand on the passenger side. I drape myself around her small frame, breathing her in, letting her clean scent – the smell of soap just unwrapped from its package – cleanse all the fissures of my soul. I transform my body into a plaster mould and imprint her on it, creating an impression of her on me.

"Christmas will come quickly," she whispers. "We'll see each other very soon."

When she lets go of me, I have a sinking feeling like I have fallen out of time.

I'm sitting in my living room drinking the tea Ganesh abandoned. Without sugarcane syrup it's bland, like a cheap, watered-down version of the real thing. But the aroma is potent and breathing it is restful.

I sink deeper into the couch, dropping my head over the backrest like someone getting their hair washed in a salon. And that's when I feel it – a hand on my shoulder. The sensation is real enough for me to jump up, terrified, but all I see behind the couch is an unadorned wall the colour of dry bone. And yet my shoulder carries a memory of the hand, its familiar smallness and warmth. Suddenly I'm filled with a lightness of spirit and aware of the irreplaceable joy of this moment, what it might mean. Are my eyes growing eyes? I'm open to all that is possible.

Katherine Fawcett

THE PULL OF OLD RAT CREEK

www.geomagneticphenomenon.ca

According to the Canadian Space Weather Prediction Centre (CSWPC), solar flares associated with geomagnetic storms in the current 11-year sun cycle (not as strong as the unprecedented 1959 space-weather events, but certainly more intense, at least initially, than the flare of 2003) produced an electromagnetic coronal mass ejection (CME) from the sun's surface on 03/04/2016. NASA monitored the cloud of charged solar particles as it travelled the approximately 150 million km from sun to earth. Although cosmic dispersion minimized global impact when the CME burst into earth's magnetic field on 03/07/2016 at 18:22 Pacific Standard Time, powerful, concentrated electromagnetic fluctuations in the troposphere were directed over a single point in a sparsely populated location in south-central British Columbia. Satellite images indicate the nearest population centre to be Old Rat Creek (pop 2558). Town officials did not record any disturbances in power grids, radio communication, or GPS.

CN Rail
Confidential Health and Safety Incident File, M. Perkins
Released in accordance with The Canadian Freedom of
Information Act
08/13/2016

Margery Perkins, 40, Assistant Manager of Paint at the Old Rat Creek Hardware store was walking along the (decommissioned) 754-B railway line between 18:00 and 18:30 on Friday, March 7, 2016. She was eating a takeout Big Juan Burrito (extra spicy) from Los Quatros Amigos Cantina wrapped in aluminum foil. Her purse contained six Hersey's Kisses, nine bobby pins, a pair of nail clippers, a tube of Dermalove psoriasis cream, and a copy of *Ten Things a Recovering Alcoholic Needs to Know in Order to Stay Sober*. She wore small hoop earrings (sterling silver) and a gold chain with a tiny locket (gold-plated) that read "Mom." The oldest of her five silver (amalgam) fillings (upper left, second bicuspid, circa 1989) was partially cracked and needed replacement.

On a separate track, approximately 2.3 km from where Ms. Perkins was walking, two freight trains, one loaded with iron ore (southbound), the other with magnetic (coking) coal (northbound), passed each other. (Because it was a single-track line, one train – in this case the one containing the iron ore – waited in the siding.) Their overlap occurred between 18:21 and 18:23.

Ms. Perkins later told medical personnel she had looked at her watch at 6:22 p.m., at the same time as she bit down on what she thought was a piece of corn tortilla wrap from the burrito, but in fact was an approximately 2 cm section of aluminum foil. The foil became temporarily lodged in the crack of her broken filling. A nerve was engaged, and a bolt of pain shot up the side of her head. The pain distracted her and caused her to lose her balance. She fell backwards, dropped the Big Juan onto a railway tie, hit her head on the metal rail and apparently lost consciousness. Vibrations from the passing iron ore car and the magnetic coal car would have travelled along the track. The aluminum foil-amalgam filling nerve corruption, combined with the concentrated electromagnetic fluctuations instigated by recorded solar activity and the energy of the passing railcars (transmitted through the line into Ms. Perkins' body) appears to have caused substantial changes to her ionic composition at the molecular level.

It is impossible to measure the physiological impact (if any) of electrical impulses from her cellphone, which rang (ringtone: Radar) 15 times before she regained consciousness. The caller, Naomi McFadden, (46, soapmaker) did not leave a voice message, but sent two text messages. The first read simply "TGIF," and was followed by an emoticon of a dancing Latino woman in long red dress. The second read, "Disco for Jesus. It's Singles Mingle Night at my church. You in?"

Tyler Shapiro, 33, percussionist for the local band Satan's Ballsack, was riding his bike along the railway tracks and discovered Ms. Perkins lying with the left side of her head on the railroad track at 18:40 p.m. She was conscious but disoriented. ("Staring into space. There was some drool," he reported.) Once Ms. Perkins was able to walk without dizziness, Mr. Shapiro accompanied her to the Rat Creek Clinic where she was treated for a mild concussion and sent home.

— Compiled with files from Rat Creek Clinic Patient Admission Report, CN Rail incident report, Smile Bright! Dentistry, iPhone records (from Apple Inc.), and Tyler Shapiro's "A Drummer's Day" blog.

Rat Creek Walk-In Medical Clinic, March 7, 2016
Patient: Margery Perkins
Address: Unit 9, 2975 Pine Grove Lane,
Old Rat Creek, BC, V0N 2K8
BC CareCard Personal Health No: 3498 480 292

Presenting symptoms: mild concussion.
Pupils: slightly dilated.
Level of consciousness: coherent.
Headache: present, not acute.
BP: 145/90 – within range
Heart rate: 71 BPM – within range.
Patient released at 21:22.

Note of Interest: Metal instruments (stethoscope, medical pen-
light, arm of reflex hammer) appear to be slightly drawn to
patient's skin, causing great interest among staff. No voiced complaints.

Magic Mini Whiteboard Message

Mom, I made a pizza. You missed my soccer game. I'm sleeping
over at Felix's.
love Owen.
PS we lost 3-1.

22

Email Message
From: Margery
To: Doug
March 8, 8:15 AM

Hi Doug,
Sorry but I slipped walking home yesterday and whacked my noggin on the train track. Had to go to the clinic. Ok if I take today off?
– M

sent from my iPhone

The Weekly Ratter
LOCAL REAL ESTATE MARKET PLUMMETS
Debbie Riley, Staff Writer

Since the closing of BritCo United Pulp and Paper Mill in January, a move that put 120 Rat Creek and area residents out of work, the number of houses on the market in the town of Rat Creek and the Rat Creek Regional District has quadrupled. Some desperate homeowners are asking 25-30% lower than assessed market value.

"It's a good time to buy," said realtor Suzanne Prescott. "People are dropping their prices. They're desperate. They're willing to take a loss just to finalize a sale."

Gary Darkhorse, a former millwright said, "That mine closing was a grave blow to the whole town. I don't know if we're ever going to get our mojo back."

***TELUS   8:23 AM   72%
Messages   Naomi   Details

You missed a good Singles Mingle last night
Pastor Kirk was asking about you.

Doubt that.

It's True!
Where were you?

Not feeling good.
Still in bed.

Don't tell me…

NO. Not hungover.

Cause if so, I would have to kill you.

I know.

Wanna go for coffee? donuts? chat?

Not today. Maybe next week.
Remember: there's no chemical solution to a spiritual problem.

Email Message
From: Doug
To: Margery
March 8, 8:31 AM

Hope you're feeling better quickly. I figure it'll be slow again today so take er easy. I'll get Norm to cover Paint for you. See you tomorrow.

—D

PS I trust we're not getting back into old habits…

sent from my iPhone

Magic Mini Whiteboard Message

Dear Owen,
Sorry about missing your game. Doug had me and Norm stay late to do inventory. I'm taking the day off to catch up on my sleep. Exhausted! Later gator.
Love, Mom

www.askarealscientist.com
Can People Really Become Magnetic?
Posted in The British Society of Skeptics (Spring 2016 Newsletter)
Tags: magnetic people, charisma, pseudoscience, skepticism, sticky people

People sometimes wonder: Is there such a thing as a magnetic person? Of course, we're not talking about someone with a magnetic personality, someone who is charismatic and attracts attention wherever they go. It's true that individuals can have magnetic personalities, even if they don't really do anything to deserve the attention or attraction.

No. We're talking about people who claim their body generates a strong magnetic field. Supporters of pseudoscience and the occult would say Yes! Of course people can become magnetic. Long live Magneto!

But well-informed skeptics and bonafide scientists know that these claims are rubbish. There is no scientific basis for a person becoming magnetic. A gaussmeter will register zero and you'll know: it's just a trick.

Click on this video link to see for yourself what these charlatans are claiming:
www.humanmagnets.com

It's obvious that all these supposedly "magnetic" people are leaning backwards slightly. Even the elderly Asian man with the iron on his chest is merely balancing it there. And who among us hasn't breathed on a spoon and had it stick to his or her nose? It's the warm vapour! That woman in the video with the coins and razor blades stuck flat to her back? Take a close look. See that sheen? She's clammy all over! Dust her with baby powder and see if that ten pence still sticks to the underside of her arm. It's a scientific fact that some people just have plain old sticky skin.

Try this: approach a supposedly magnetic person with a compass. If they are truly magnetic, the compass will go spinning wildly off in all directions. If not? Tell that person he/she needs a shower.

Happy Campers Canada!
Order Confirmation # 98470948

One (1) Silva Explorer Compass
Ordered on: March 10, 2016, 10:55 AM
Purchased by: M. Perkins
Shipping Address: Unit 9, 2975 Pine Grove Lane, Old Rat Creek, BC, V0N 2K8

The Silva Explorer Compass keeps you and your buddies on course while you are hiking, hunting or just exploring. Two-degree gradations and declination scales make it easy for you to plot a precise path. This compass comes with a sturdy lanyard, so you can wear it around your neck to keep it within easy reach. Also included is a magnifier, which makes this outdoor compass easy to read.

Cost: $18.00
Delivery charge: $7.95 (ships in 7-9 business days).
Payment Method: VISA **** **** **** 1021, expiry date 09/18

Email Message
From: Doug
To: Margery
March 13, 9:30 PM

I forgot to check before you left today about that gaussmeter you were after. Did you mean one of those thingamabobs that measure magnetic flux density? The last time we had a request for a gaussmeter was when those high school kids were having a seance and they thought they could detect paranormal energy. You going ghost-busting?

sent from my iPhone

The Donut Hole: Incident Report
Employee: Todd Hewson
Shift Manager: Ken Trunkle
March 14, 2016, 4:00 p.m. (approx.)

Two women seated at Table 12 (actually a booth) started doing this weird thing with spoons. I recognized them because they are regulars and also one of them goes to church with my mom. One lady was patting the other lady with spoons, all over her. Like tapping her, slowly. Then she would kind of let go and the spoons were sticking on her, even when she stood up. Then they started doing it with forks too. And knives. They must have had some kind of glue or invisible tape or it was a thing with static electricity. At one point there were approximately 15 or 20 spoons and forks and knives on the one lady, hanging from her arms and legs and back and front and even on her face.

Naturally, I suspected they were going to steal them. Thinking of our meeting of last month re: utensil loss, I told the Shift Manager (Ken) to check it out and he did. He said (and I quote) that was the most fucked-uppest thing he'd ever seen. Then he told me to do this incident report while he went over there and told the ladies to put the utensils back. They did. Then they left.

The Weekly Ratter
TOURISM IS OUR ONLY HOPE, SAYS MAYOR
Local Economy on Steep Decline
Debbie Riley, Staff Writer

With five local businesses closing their doors in the past 30 days, Old Rat Creek Mayor Bill Willson says the area needs tourist dollars to revitalize the economy and lift residents' spirits. He says bringing visitors to town is essential to re-establish a robust economy and save the businesses that remain.

Willson encourages residents to post "awesome pictures of how awesome our town can be" on social media. "We're living in a tourist-driven economy. Whistler's got their ski hill and what have you. Kelowna's got vineyards. But the people of Rat Creek are really friendly, and the scenery is awesome. The trees! The fields! The creek! We've just got to get the word out. Call your friends! Call your family! Tell 'em we're friendly! Tell 'em it's beautiful here!"

Chamber of Commerce and Tourism Board officials will be meeting next Wednesday (March 29) to discuss strategies for an economic enhancement plan. Public input is encouraged.

iPhone transcription of registered user M. Perkins
March 15, 2016, 3:09 PM
Apple Privacy Centre, Toronto, ON, Canada

Margery: Can a concussion cause body changes?
Siri: I'm not sure I understand.
Margery: Why do I feel pulled towards metal objects?
Siri: Interesting question.
Margery: Why do I feel a pull towards metal objects?
Siri: Interesting question.
Margery: I'm going crazy.
Siri: There's no need for that.
Margery: Do fat people attract metal?
Siri: Let's see. Here's what I found on the web for 'Do fat people attract metal' Are women attracted to fat men?
www.peertrainer.com;
Fat Bottom Girls, heavy metal remix www.queenrocks.com;
Why do I attract fat people? www.answers.yahoo.com
Margery: If I stay in bed all day will this condition go away?
Siri: Let's see. Here's what I found on the web for 'If I stay in bed all day, will this condition go away?' Why do depressed people lie in bed? www.psychdoctor.com;
Bedrest: Does it help your condition? www.mommieslife.com;
How to recover from sleeping all day. www.woeisme.org;
Get fired up in bed! www.spiceitup.com
Margery: You are no help at all.
Siri: I am?

Margery: Maybe I do need a drink.

Siri: Ok – check it out. Here's what I found on the web for licensed restaurants near you: The Woodcutter, 1436 Canoe Landing; Pony Bar and Grill, 65 Main Street.

Magic Mini Whiteboard Message

Mom,

Have you seen my saxophone? It's not in the case and I need it for band tomorrow.

Love Owen

***TELUS   11:31 PM   38%
Messages   Naomi   Details

Still happening?

> *yup.*

So weird!

> *yup.*

Ever think it might be a sign from God?

> *nope.*

*Seriously. Like people who get
visions of Mother Mary on their toast.
Or start bleeding from their hands. Like it's
the wounds of Jesus from getting nailed to
the cross.*

> *Naomi, I have paper clips
> all over me. Maybe it's a sign
> from Office Depot.*

I don't think you're taking it seriously.

>*oh, i am taking it seriously.*
>*I'm seeing Dr. Payne on Monday*

Maybe it's a heavenly gift, and you are
meant to use it for good in the world.
You should pray for an answer.

>*How about you pray,*
>*i'll go see doc.*
>*gnite.*

God bless

The Weekly Ratter

LOCAL WOMAN SAVES DAY WITH MAGNETIC POWER

Grandpa can get back on his Harley
by Debbie Riley, staff writer

When Jim Cole's father lost his motorcycle key on Monday, he thought he might be stuck in the BC interior forever. He never dreamed that a human magnet would save the day.

But that's exactly what happened when Jim Cole Sr., who had stopped for a visit with his son's family while en route from Edmonton to Langley, dropped the key for his Harley Davidson 2002 Sportster somewhere in West Hills Park picnic area during a family barbecue.

"That key was lost somewhere between the woods behind the outhouse and the parking lot," said the younger Cole. "It could have been in the grass, in the gravel, in the dirt. Anywhere! And he didn't have a spare."

The Coles had been searching for over an hour, when it seemed their prayers were answered.

"This woman was walking by and asked what we were doing. Well, when we told her we'd lost that key, she just took her Crocs off and slowly walked around the park and I'll be damned if the key didn't stick right to her foot. It was over in the weeds by the doggie-doo bag dispenser. She also found $4.25 in loonies and quarters, a few bottle caps, and one earring."

Jim Cole, Sr. was able to get to Langley on schedule. "Sure, I love visiting family in your town, but nobody likes to feel stranded," he said during a telephone interview. "Who knows how long we would've been out there on our hands and knees if that lady hadn't shown up. We invited her to stay for a hot dog and a beer, but she said she was on off to a doctor's appointment."

The woman's identity could not be confirmed.

Alexander MacKenzie High School physics and biology teacher Richard Wiggins said there is no such thing as a human with magnetic power. He said the woman likely had a metal detector hidden in the leg of her pants.

Email Message
From: Dr. E. Payne GP, Old Rat Creek Medical Centre
To: Dr. Morgan, Endocrinologist, North Vancouver
April 5, 2016, 1:43 PM

<u>Margery Perkins</u> ("Patient") is experiencing unnatural attraction to metal. (Tested in examining room with coins, thumbtacks and a variety of steel diagnostic instruments.) No pain associated with attraction. Unprecedented in my clinical experience. Also presents: mild asthma, tooth sensitivity, psoriasis on upper arms. Mildly obese. See attached blood tests.

Signed, ———————————————

Dr. Emily Payne, by email.

Magic Mini Whiteboard Message

Mom, where is all the change from my money jar? Only the bills and some American coins are still there. And I found my sax in your room…since when do you play?
love Owen

Old Rat Creek Community Forum
Facebook Post
April 19, 2016, 7:45 PM

To the lady who was crossing at the intersection of Frontier and Arbutus:

I am so sorry! This has never happened before. I didn't get a chance to apologize before you dashed off, but seriously it was as if my bike had a mind of its own. I came at you like there was a wind that blew me into you. I hope you're okay, and I want you to know that it wasn't my fault. Lucky for me my carbon-fibre frame wasn't damaged!

If our town planners thought about making a bike lane for non-emitting commuters, maybe this kind of accident wouldn't happen!

Hello Old Rat Creek town council???

Please share if you support cyclists!

April 23, 2016
From the desk of Dr. A. Morgan,
Endocrinologist, North Vancouver, BC
Re: Margery Perkins, Old Rat Creek

Patient reports physical attraction toward iron, steel and nickel.
Endocrine system within range, including adrenals, pituitary, pineal, thyroid, parathyroid.
Possible anemia.
Suggestion: Increase consumption of leafy greens, legumes, red meat.
Further testing required.

***TELUS   6:42 PM   38%
Messages   Naomi   Details

Can I ask you a favour?

Of course

And as my BFF and former sponsor,
promise you won't think I'm weird?

I'm still your sponsor. Always will be.
And I already think you're weird.
What's up?

I'm having some issues with my lower back.
Easy. Need a massage?

Not exactly.

Coins stuck where you can't reach again?

Ha ha.
I only put them in reachable places now.

Good.

> *But I do need you to come over*
> *and run an iron up and down my spine.*

?????

> *Don't have to plug it in.*
> *Don't have to heat it up.*
> *Just iron places I can't reach.*
> *Hello?*
> *Hello?*

ya, I can do that.

> *thank-you. Its kinda urgent.*

OK. I'm bringing Pastor Kirk. He really likes you.
And is totally non-judgemental.

Magic Mini Whiteboard Message

Dear Owen,
Oh yeah, sorry about the $$. I needed change for parking. Returned it today in bills. You had $45 in quarter, loonies and toonies in there!
love Mom

Voice mail recording from 604-966-****

Hi Margery, it's me, Jennifer! We met on the Greyhound when you were going to your doctor's appointment a while back. Remember? Anywho, it was great to chat. Like I was saying, mainstream medical industry doesn't always have our best interests at heart. That acupuncturist I was trying to remember is Dr.

Jian Chen. He's the real deal. Helped me with my fibroids. Google C-H-E-N Acupuncture. You don't have to call me back. Good luck! Bye!

from The AA Big Book:
The Serenity Prayer

God grant me the serenity to accept the things I cannot change,
the courage to change the things I can,
and the wisdom to know the difference

www.unclescottsMSFsupplies.com
UNCLE SCOTT'S MAGNETIC SHIELDING FOIL AND SUPPLIES
"America's Best Material Available for Shielding DC, ELF & VLF Magnetic Fields" ...and great service too!

Industry experts have trusted Uncle Scott to shield delicate electronic components from EMFs for years! And now, this flexible magnetic Shielding Foil made of 80% nickel alloy can be yours at affordable prices for your personal home or business use. Choose from thinner material that can be easily trimmed with ordinary kitchen scissors and shaped by hand, or our thicker material, which offers higher shielding performance (requires Tin Snips to cut).

Use our unique Shielding Foil to create a magnetic barrier for your doorbell transformer, cellphone, microwave oven, buried wiring, and more. You can expect as much as 82% attenuation of the magnetic field with one layer of thickness (providing the shield is snug fitting). Multiple layers can be used for even greater reduction.

NOTE: We recommend using a gaussmeter to determine the exact shape and positioning of the magnetic shield, and to confirm that the magnetic fields have been reduced to desired levels.

CAUTION: Shielding Foil has sharp edges! Please use extreme caution when cutting.

Magnetic Shielding Foil: 15" wide, 0.003" thick (# N785-3) $27.95/linear ft. [add to cart]

Magnetic Shielding Foil: 15" wide, 0.011" thick (# N785-4) $33.95/linear ft. [add to cart]

Magic Mini Whiteboard Message

Mom, this town is SOOOOOO BORING AND DEAD. Me and Felix are thinking of moving to Vancouver after graduation. Love Owen

Email Message
From: Doug
To: Margery
May 10, 11:30 AM

Margery, this has got to stop. I don't care what you do in your spare time (you know that) but now it's starting to really affect your work. Norm saw you wrapping the grade 30-proof coil chain (the stuff w/ hot galvanized finish) around your waist and draping it over your shoulders in the break room yesterday. He thought it was some kind of bondage/S&M thing. People are starting to talk! Margery, you're not doing a very good job "hiding" this so-called "affliction." I've told you time and time again to keep your hands out of the screws. It's bad enough when you are always pressing yourself against the shelving.

– D

sent from my iPhone

***TELUS	6:42 PM	38%
Messages	**Naomi**	**Details**

Can I come to church with you?

Of course!

Couldn't hurt to get a little direction I suppose.

*God will be delighted to see a
heathen like you ha ha. So will
Pastor Kirk.*

*I'm not interested in the Pastor,
and I don't think God's interested in me.*

*"Do not fear, for I am with you. Do
not be dismayed, for I am your God.
I will strengthen you and help you; I will uphold
you with my righteous right hand." (Isaiah, 41:10)*

*I got stuck to the side of
a delivery van yesterday.
Had to get Doug to pull me off.*

I'll pick you up…

Thanks

Wait: do you mean for Sunday morning in the sanctuary,
or Wednesday evening in the basement?

Ah, ye of little faith.
Sunday!

See you at 9:45.

Jian Chen's Family Acupuncture Clinic
Richmond, BC

(private and confidential)

Memo to All Staff:
Because of an incident last month in our Cook Road clinic, treatment rooms will now be equipped with emergency pliers. Please remember that if a needle enters the tissue smoothly and without resistance, this indicates an energy meridian. However, if a needle appears to be *pulled* or *sucked* in any way *into* the body of a patient, the procedure must be stopped immediately and Dr. Chen must be alerted.

It is your responsibility to familiarize yourself with the use of the pliers.
Xie-xie,
Mrs. Chen

Dear Ms. Perkins,
I, along with the members of the clergy here at Rat Creek Apostolic Church, would like to thank you for the unique offering-cum-special event after last Sunday's worship service in

the sanctuary. When Naomi McFadden tossed that loonie at you and it stuck on your (lovely) dress, we all thought it was some kind of prank! We thought there must be some adhesive quality to the coin. But when the seniors put down their teacups and began rummaging through their wallets for change to toss at you, we knew that a Holy Presence had been delivered. Never has the congregation had such fun with their offerings!

Please accept my apologies for Mrs. Henry. At 91-years-old, even though her hearing is just about gone, her throwing arm seems to get stronger and stronger. I hope the swelling in your forehead went down quickly.

I was delighted that the youngsters, who normally spend Community Sharing Time drinking juice and eating Digestive Biscuits and sliding around in their stocking feet downstairs, all came up to see what was going on. Of course, they asked their parents for money to toss. Praise God, indeed. Although unortho-dox, it was certainly appreciated.

If you are so moved, I would be delighted to discuss making the Sunday Coin Toss a regular event at Rat Creek Apostolic Church.

Sincerely,
Pastor Kirk Bedrock

PS: I hope you enjoyed my sermon on Accepting Miracles. How timely! That $182 will be put to good use in God's name.

PPS: Ms. McFadden probably already told you, but it's Hip Hop Hallelujah next Friday here. Hope you can make it! Singles Mingle nights are really a gas.

Magic Mini Whiteboard Message

Dear Owen,
Moving? Vancouver?
Town's in a slump, but these things come and go. Let's talk tomorrow.
Love, Mom

PS After our chat the other day, I'm trying to see this thing between me and metal as a gift. Just have to figure out how to put it to good use.

Happy Campers Canada! Customer Relations
June 1, 2016
Re: Online Order Confirmation # 98470948:
Thank you for your recent correspondence.

We are sorry that your recent order of <u>One (1) Silva Explorer Compass</u> (March 10, 2016) is <u>not satisfactory</u>. At Happy Campers Canada! (online division) we are proud to offer a full refund on any merchandise returned in the original packaging.

Please note that we have never had a customer report of one of our compasses "spinning wildly off in all directions" before.

Once the merchandise <u>One (1) Silva Explorer Compass </u>is received by Happy Campers Canada! a full refund will be credited to VISA cardholder **** **** **** 1021

Customer satisfaction is our number one concern. Please feel free to contact us if we can be of further assistance.

"Go Play Outside!"

Facebook Messenger
Margery,
I thought I'd send you this. Found it on www.youatewhat.com
Top 10 Strange Cravings
1. Ice
2. Toothpaste
3. Coal
4. Sponges
5. Dirt
6. Chalk
7. Newspapers
8. Matches (cardboard, with sulphur tip)
9. Starch
10. Rubber (erasers, balloons, elastic bands) (tires excluded.)

Other strange cravings that people reported include bricks, laundry soap and raw sausages. Doesn't mean there's no one else in the world who craves metal and thinks about gulping down a ball bearing now and then. But I don't think it's safe. Lick it – sure. Don't see the harm, as long as it's clean. Swallow it? No. Don't do it. Just like before, if you feel the urges getting so strong you don't think you can fight them alone, call. I'm here for you – Naomi

June 9, 2016
Bird World Weekly

Thousands of migratory birds – including waterfowl (ducks and geese), raptors (hawks and eagles), wading birds (cranes, herons, gulls, terns, and shorebirds,) and songbirds (sparrows, warblers, blackbirds, and thrushes) – known to be on their north-south migratory path have been observed by Western Canadian ornithologists flying in easterly-westerly directions. Reports to the British Columbia Bird Observation Centre (BC-BOC) since mid-May suggest that V-formations, which normally would be headed to Canada's North, have been colliding with each other, lead-bird first, over a sparsely populated area of central British Columbia.

University of Victoria zoology professor Jeremy Pyck said that although surprisingly little is understood about the neuronal substrates which support migratory birds' extraordinary navigational ability, the planet's magnetic field appears to be the primary (but not sole) orientation cue.

"Migratory birds are genetically programmed to fly a certain direction, based on geomagnetic pull. They aren't like puppies. They don't just fly higgledy-piggledy. This east-west flight pattern we're observing in some areas of BC really is unprecedented and suggests a kind of migratory path confusion. These birds are lost."

Wild Canada spokesperson Amber Rainbow said the tar sands activity is to blame.

<June 10, 2016>
Private and confidential
Margery Perkins
Dear <Ms Perkins,>

<u>Notice of Termination</u>

I am writing to inform you of the termination of your employment with <Old Rat Creek Hardware.>

During our meeting of <May 9, 2016> you were advised that targets for <not walking around with metal hardware stuck to you> were not being met, and that <safety/conformity standards were being compromised.>

<On May 21> you had a second meeting with me. Also present were Tim Arnaud (Light Fixtures), Hannah Point (Seasonal), and Norm Went (Lumber). You were advised that your overall <not being magnetic> had not improved to the level required. In that meeting you were issued with a final warning letter. This letter indicated that your employment may be terminated if the aforementioned issue did not improve by <insert date>.

We consider that your <not being magnetic> is still unsatisfactory and have decided to terminate your employment for failure to comply with standards of on-the-job expectations. Your employment will end immediately. In lieu of receiving two weeks' notice, you will be paid the sum of $<1,862.00>, which includes accrued entitlements and outstanding remuneration, up to and including your last day of employment.

Yours sincerely,
Mr. Douglas Armstrong,
Manager, Old Rat Creek Hardware.
C.C. Marty Stye, Independent Hardware Inc., Head Office

Email message
From: Doug
To: Margery
June 10, 11:40 PM

Jeez M, I'm sorry about that letter but I had to put it in writing to make it official for head office, and that was the only template we had on file. My hands are tied. Frankly, Margery, I'm concerned about you. I've kept you on through "rough patches" before, but this involves knives, drill bits and saws. Not only are you putting yourself at risk working here, but we'd be liable as a company if you got hurt while on shift.

I know you explained how the stuff doesn't come at you pointy end first, but I *do* worry. And now you're not even wearing the Crocs or rubber gloves or that neoprene wetsuit under your uniform like you did at first. It's affecting your ability to work. It's affecting relationships with co-workers. Norm thinks your body was replaced by aliens! (I don't know if he was joking or not. Remember his crop circle theories?) But you must admit, whatever's going on with you is pretty hard to explain scientifically.

In any case, it's affecting sales. Business here has slowed down enough as it is. Remember last month's Up With Hardware meeting, where we talked about how everyone has to go above and beyond with customer service? Well, sorry to say it, but no one wants to "pluck" a piece of hardware off of you. "The hinge you're looking for is stuck to the underside of my arm" just doesn't cut it, Margery.

This isn't "personal" and of course I will write you a formal letter of reference! I think you'd be great somewhere like a store that sells wool or something. Or wicker furniture. And, yes, (sorry I didn't get back to you on this earlier), you can certainly order that Magnetic Shielding Foil from Uncle Scott's through the store – I'll run it in through my personal account so you can still get staff discount. I think that's a great step. Fashion yourself a little "suit of armour." I'll give you a call when it arrives.

Cheers,
– D

Magic Mini Whiteboard Message

Dear Mom,
Well, Felix said I could stay with him 'til exams are done and we can leave. Because the way you're acting now, it's worse than when you were a drunk.

A spaghetti pot on your head? Hello?

I don't care whether it's a disease, a choice, or a "gift." I'm gonna get a normal job in a normal place like a normal person.

Owen.

Old Rat Creek Police Department, Incidents Report

Case #2016-295034
Incident Type: Exposure
Incident Date: 06/27/2016, 2:15 AM

Incident Address: 200 block Pine St.

Arrested: Margery L. Perkins, age 40, of Unit 9, 2975 Pine Grove Lane, Old Rat Creek, BC

Suspect was arrested for: <u>Lewd, Lascivious Behaviour in a Public Place</u>.

Details: The ORCPD, with information obtained by reports from passersby, arrested Ms. Margery Perkins for lewd behaviour as she was curled inside a corrugated steel culvert (diameter, 0.85 meters) near town hall, without clothing. When asked to explain herself, Ms. Perkins pressed her tongue against the culvert and began muttering. Her words were incomprehensible.

Ms. Perkins was released on $200.00 bail to the custody of Pastor Kirk Bedrock, who brought her a blanket and promised to arrange some form of community service as restitution.

Notice to Quit
July 2, 2016

NOTICE TO: Margery Perkins, TENANT in possession and all others

TAKE NOTICE THAT:

Pursuant to a written lease (the "Lease") dated Jan. 1, 2004, you are a tenant for the premises described as: Unit 9, Shady Acres, 2975 Pine Grove Lane, Old Rat Creek, BC, ("The Premises") of which you now hold possession.

On June 22, 2016, during routine maintenance, it was discovered that the Tenant had:

1. removed door from refrigerator in unit, and placed it on the bedroom floor. A foul odour emanated from the food remaining on the fridge shelves.

1a. accumulated a substantial number of landscaping tools and items from the Caretaker's Shed (including but not limited to: spades, rakes, trowels and large steel hedge trimmer).

2. between June 3 and June 22 2016, The Landlord received no less that twelve (12) complaints from Shady Acres residents about The Tenant's behaviour. Complaints include but are not limited to:

2a. sprawling over the hoods of various parked cars in the (common) Parking Area,

2b. climbing on the metal gate in the (common) Courtyard Area, and

2c. physically blocking Mail Box access in the (common) Foyer.

Due to said damages and/or actions by you and/or your guests, The Landlord hereby elects to terminate The Lease. You are given at least thirty (30) days notice to quit the premises in compliance with the applicable laws in the Province of British Columbia. Accordingly, The Tenant must vacate and surrender the Premises to The Landlord by noon on August 2, 2016.

THIS NOTICE TO QUIT IS GIVEN PURSUANT TO THE APPLICABLE LAWS OF THE PROVINCE OF BRITISH COLUMBIA AND IN NO WAY IMPAIRS OR LIMITS ANY OF THE OTHER REMEDIES OR RIGHTS THAT THE LANDLORD MAY HAVE UNDER THE LEASE OR UNDER SAID LAWS

iPhone transcription of registered user M. Perkins, July 2, 2016,
3:09 PM
Apple Privacy Centre, Toronto, ON, Canada

Margery: Why is this happening to me?
Siri: Here's what I found on the web for 'Why is this happening to me?'
www.whyisthishappening.net Simple ways to reduce failure and increase positive energy;
www.whyme.org Free Audiobook
Margery: Is this one of those things I can't change?
Siri: Okay. I found this on the web for 'Is this one of those things I can't change?' www.quoted.com The wheel of change moves on, and those who were up go down and those…;
www.thechangeinyou.com 15 Things You Can Do Today To Make A Positive Change
Margery: Is a large pile of metal a tourist attraction?
Siri: Here's what I found on the web for 'Is a large pile of metal a tourist attraction?'
www.roadsidewonders.com World's largest metal scarecrow, Minnesota; 20 Best Canadian Roadside Attractions: #1 The Ginormous Hockey Stick and Puck in Duncan, BC

OLD RAT CREEK BUY, SELL, TRADE ANYTHING
Closed Group

For Sale: Magnetic Shielding Foil: 15" wide, 0.011" thick.
Price: This is a steal at $10.00 OBO.
Details: Great for protecting sensitive electronic equipment from magnetic fields. You can use it to get rid of magnetic impulses. Don't need it anymore.

BONUS: I'll throw in a (gently) used gaussmeter (device for detecting electromagnetic radiation. Also used in seances and for detecting paranormal activity.)
Contact: PM Margery if interested!

Voice mail recording from 604-894-****

Hey, kiddo, it's Mom.
So, how's Vancouver? You and Felix gonna get tickets to one of those Whitecaps games?

I miss you.

I miss your messages on your silly old magic mini whiteboard. You know we've had that thing since you were three years old? I haven't erased your last one, where you said you'd try and come back and visit. I sure hope you will. It's weird around here without you. Quiet.

I guess I'm an empty nester now.
Well, take care.

Travel BC – August eNews
Odd Roadside Attractions For The Whole Family

Here's one Roadside Attraction you're sure to be attracted to!

Something amazing has popped up in the quaint little town of Old Rat Creek (Exit 5 off Highway 72). Travellers of all ages will love "Magnetic Margery," a dazzling eleven-foot tower of metal objects.

You, too, can join the fun by adding something metal to Magnetic Margery! Hey, son, why not add a little metal hot rod race car? Maybe sis wants to toss on a piece of loonie store jewelry! Mom and Dad can contribute a safety pin, a bottle cap, or a fishing lure! Let's watch the tower grow and grow as metal pieces cling to it.

Local legend has it that tossing something metallic at Magnetic Margery will bring good luck. Just like tossing coins in a fountain! People come from far and wide to add their metal pieces to this one-of-a-kind tower.

Located in BC Pioneer Heritage Park, at the intersection of Main Street and 2nd Avenue (beside the Esso). See map below.

Warning: Visitors with artificial cardiac pacemakers are advised to stay at least 20 feet from the Tower (behind yellow line). The town of Old Rat Creek is not responsible for the loss of keys, coins, metal eyeglasses, or other valuables to the tower. Metal objects you do not wish to add to Magnetic Margery should be held securely.

* The Magnetic Margery Roadside Attraction is patrolled by AA Aardvark Security 24 hours/day.

Old Rat Creek Tourism Bureau
Private Memo to Board of Directors
August 17, 2016

CONFIDENTIAL:
Volunteers are still needed to administer Margery's noon smoothie meal replacement through the plastic feeding tube. Thanks to Lilah and Jack who have tended to her for the past six weeks, to Dr. Louis, who designed her Evacuation Trough, and to the Green Hippie for providing a different flavour of organic, high-protein, meal replacement smoothie for Margery every day.

CBC News – online edition
October 14, 2016
Old Rat Creek Becomes New BC Tourist Mecca

A new hot spot has emerged on the Western Canadian tourist scene. Visitors to Old Rat Creek, BC, have made this sleepy little town, 200 km from the nearest mall, "The Place To Be," according to Tourism BC. Visitor numbers from the period between the August long weekend (BC Day) and Thanksgiving (Oct. 11) indicate approximately 31,900 people made the trip up Hwy. 72 to Old Rat Creek, putting the destination fourth (after Whistler, Tofino, and Shushwap Lake) for tourist visits.

The spike in visitors is due to the town's giant metallic "wishing tower" dubbed "Magnetic Margery." According to local lore, an unemployed, homeless, overweight, introverted single mother who suffers from alcoholism and psoriasis lives inside the tower and pulls the metal objects towards her with a magnetic force bestowed upon her by God.

Rat Creek Apostolic Church Pastor Kirk Bedrock said tourists have not only been tossing their metal objects at Magnetic Margery, they've been filling the pews every Sunday. "We haven't had attendance like this since the Canucks made the playoffs," he said. "But all kidding aside, I think we have a modern-day miracle here."

FOR IMMEDIATE RELEASE
2017 Spring/Summer Job Fair
(Sponsored by the Old Rat Creek Economic Development Department)

Come one, come all, and learn about all the employment opportunities in our booming town!

Skilled and unskilled workers needed. Bring your resumé, and bring your friends. Interviews may be conducted on the spot.

Booths will be set up at the Town Office on Saturday, May 5, from 9 a.m. - 9 p.m., with HR representatives from the following companies:
• Ye Olde Rat Creeke Fudgery
• Rat Creek Best Western
• Owen and Felix's "Whitecaps North" Indoor Soccer Training Academy
• Oh Canada, Eh? Maple Syrup and T-Shirts Retail Emporium
• Naomi's Next-To-Godliness Soap Company
• True North Performing Arts Centre
• Tim Hortons (formerly The Donut Hole)
• Canadian Tire (formerly Old Rat Creek Hardware)
And many more!

The band Iron Glory (formerly Satan's Ballsack) will be playing gospel-rock in the foyer of the Town Office all afternoon.

Old Rat Creek Community Forum
Facebook Post
June 1, 2017, 10:55 PM

— Did anybody see that lightning? — OMG, it was right over the Wishing Tower!
— That's the kind of bolt God usually saves for Saskatchewan
— Well, duh, metal attracts lightning. You people are such idiots.

The Daily Ratter
06/02/2017

A bolt of lightning struck the top of "Magnetic Margery" just before 11:00 last night, apparently causing Rat Creek's version of the Eiffel Tower to lose its magnetic quality and come crashing down. No one was injured on the outside of the tower. Emergency crews are searching for the body of Margery Perkins, who some Chamber of Commerce officials claim lived within the tower. The public is being advised to stay away from the area until further notice.

Old Rat Creek Tourism Bureau
Private Memo to Board of Directors
June 2/2017

CONFIDENTIAL:

Although rumours abound, we can confirm that the fire department, the ambulance, and the police, along with Happy Scrappy's Metal Recyclers and Bob The Welder Welding Services, were unable to find any human remains within the pile of metallic debris at Heritage Park. The investigation will continue. In the meantime, please do not speak to members of the press about this unfortunate incident. CBC, Global, CTV, and CNN have all been here snooping around. But you know what they say: All publicity is good publicity. And as Tourism Board Chair Kirk Bedrock said, "Think of what happened to religion when Jesus died!"

Don't forget, tonight is opening night for the new production at True North Performing Arts Centre (*Pine Beetle: The Musical*).

www.geomagneticphenomenon.ca

According to the Canadian Space Weather Prediction Centre (CSWPC), unprecedented levels of aurora borealis (northern lights) have been visible over central British Columbia recently. Forecasters are uncertain as to why this phenomenon is occurring; there has been no significant change in geomagnetic activity (solar flares) recently. Waves of green and purple were first reported on June 4 (23:10), and have been visible to the naked eye, even during daytime hours, since the initial observations.

Auroral activity is typically produced by the ionization and excitation of atmospheric elements (charged particles) in the magnetosphere, which then become luminescent. Lucien Valencia, a spokesperson for The International Association of Oceanic and Atmospheric Research said that, although unlikely, geomagnetic forces escaping an object, organism, or geological feature on the top layer of the earth's surface (the crust) could explain the abnormally intense display of cosmic hue.

Satellite images and first-person reports indicate the unnaturally intense cosmic phenomenona appear to be strongest near the town of Old Rat Creek, where a freak lightning bolt caused irreparable damage to a local landmark exactly three days prior to the appearance of the aurora borealis.

Delighted town officials reported that power grids, radio communication, and GPS systems in the area are working "better than ever," and they are mounting a campaign to rebrand their town as Northern Lights Capital of the World.

Western Canadian Aurora Borealis Tracker
Facebook Group – Public

Becky posted a video from Old Rat Creek, BC, June 4, 2017
138,308 views
9387 comments

— Holy crap! Great vid Becky!
— I've never seen blues and greens and PINKS like that EVER. Even when I was cross-country skiing in the Arctic Circle. This place is amazing.

— People. Wake up. Global warming brings on more intense aurora. Stop Big Oil now before this becomes our new normal.

— Did you guys see the V of geese flying through the lights? Pretty freakin cool.

— I got a gaussameter online last year. As soon as those northern lights appeared, it started beeping like nuts all day.

— OMG it was so bright and dazzling through the window my granddaughter couldn't sleep.

— So? Close the curtain old lady!

— We don't have those brilliant lights so strong even here in Iceland.

— Like God's favourite crayons were melting.

Darlene Madott

WINNERS AND LOSERS

"Good afternoon, sir."

He did not acknowledge her greeting, though she was standing right behind him in the Stratford theatre ticket lineup, though they had spent the last two weeks together, on opposite sides of the courtroom, litigating the same case. Was it possible he didn't see her? So, when she repeated the greeting and he maintained his silence, she felt mortified.

Throughout the first week of the divorce trial, at almost every break, John Jeremey Johnston, Q.C., had rubbed shoulders with her, a collegial prodding: "C'mon, we can settle this."

"No, we can't. Your client should shelve her libido and raise the kids in close proximity to their father. Then we can talk."

But no, his client, Cindy Lampe, had fallen in love with a bus driver, Joe Blanchard, on the run from Toronto to Thunder Bay. No compromise was available. John Jeremey Johnston, Q.C., with his army of junior lawyers and articling students accompanying him daily to the trial, reasoned that the parent-child relationship was sustainable by taking away during-the-week time and tacking this onto Christmas and summer holidays – same net time. Out came his maps and travel times, and testimonies as to how quickly a motivated parent could traverse the distance between Toronto and Thunder Bay.

Her argument was simple. Time is not fungible. There is no substitute for the availability of a father – in this case, Al Lampe – on a moment's notice. How do you pick up a sick kid from school and home to Nanna for chicken soup for lunch, between Toronto and Thunder Bay?

What made her advocacy successful was not that she was better than her learned friend, but that she *believed* in what she advocated – the importance of a present parent to a child, all that stands between the child and the darkness.

~~~

"You see this," she had told her young son, Marco, opening the freezer door the weekend before the trial to show him the President's Choice frozen dinners. She had pointed to the written instructions on the packaging. "As long as you can read, you will never starve." She had shown Marco how to turn on the oven, had given him the keys to their home.

The first night of the trial, struggling home with her briefcases at 8:00 o'clock in the evening, she had come in to the smell of shepherd's pie, a candle lit for her on the dining room table, a glass of wine poured, her son practicing the piano.

"Do I have to do this all over again, tomorrow, Momma?"

The second day of trial, her secretary had walked across Bond Street to St. Michael's Choir School to pick up Marco from the playground and put him in a cab for home – this time with Chinese take-out on his lap. Toward the end of the first week, he'd found his own way home, by subway and then bus, starting his journey with the older boys from the Choir School, growing independence as he facilitated his mother's work, the two of them making a team together, helping each other survive the ordeal of this trial.

The last night of the trial, she had stayed at the office until 1:00 o'clock in the morning, writing the closing argument she would hand up to the judge the next day, in bound form and on a memory stick, using her computer throughout the trial, where

John Jeremey Johnston, Q.C. had used his juniors and students. She had kept calling home, urging her son to go to bed. But Marco had remained up, all the lights on, waiting for his mother, of an age when it was illegal for a parent to leave a child at home alone, untended. Sometimes risks had to be taken. Marco knew that his Momma would come home. He knew that, unfailingly.

She had to feel the human grip in every case before she could take on the fight. She honestly believed that parenting took sacrifice, that even a separated mother doesn't get to just move away. A mother has to be there. At the very least, a father has to be able to get there, to be on immediate call. Separation requires teamwork. The intensity with which she litigated her cases, she had been told, crossed boundaries, was unprofessional.

"You take the law too seriously." It wasn't the law about which she cared. It was men and women, caught up in the vortex of their personal dramas. She had never learned to not take her cases personally.

∾

"Good afternoon, sir."

Nothing.

She would never have expected this of John Jeremey Johnston, Q.C., and certainly not here, in the Stratford ticket retrieval line-up. On this day, of all days? The day after his defeat at the hands of herself, a junior counsel.

∾

After the trial, she had ridden her bike downtown, to clean up her office and get on top of her other work that had accumulated over two weeks. Marco was with his father for the weekend. Work had been the only way she ever knew how to staunch the pain of her own separation, spending every alternating Saturday and Sunday working twelve-hour days until the weekend would be over and Marco returned. But inside her office, on this particular Saturday morning, she could take working no longer. She thought she would suffocate.

She left the bike in the office, and walked to Dundas Square. Impulsively, she ordered a rush ticket to *All's Well that Ends Well*, and then a bus ticket to Stratford.

It was on the bus to Stratford that she learned there would be no same-day return. She would be free, therefore, to stay in Stratford for the weekend.

Her biggest problem in the world became where to stay.

A fellow passenger overheard her distress and gave her the phone number for the Stratford Board of Trade. While still on the bus, she found a bed and breakfast with availability, noted the hours for the bus departing Stratford for Toronto on Sunday, placing her back home seamlessly in time to greet her returning son.

And then at the start of the afternoon performance, on the outside balcony of the theatre, glass of white wine in hand under a spectacular sky, the trumpets heralded the audience to the play – a sudden rush of euphoria. Harming no one, she had just run away. No one knew where she was. She had her cellphone and a credit card. No one would be looking for her. She had never felt this free.

It was as if she did not exist.

And then, she did not exist.

John Jeremey Johnston, Q.C. was shaming her. But not for having won. No. He was shaming her – she was sure – because of that moment of *his* humiliation in the courtroom, a moment caused by an unwitting answer made by her client, Al Lampe.

To prepare Al for cross-examination, she had asked him what was the absolute worst thing Cindy, the mother of his children, would say about him as a father and a human being.

John Jeremey Johnston, Q.C., large in professional reputation, though not in size, had been honing in during his cross-examination. Anticipating his next question, Al had said:

"You're going to ask me about those strip clubs on the Queensway, where I took my clients to entertain them. Cindy needn't have worried. Cindy had no concerns about the strip clubs, sir, because – well, sir – men of yours and my stature, we're not very attractive to women."

It was spoken so respectfully and wholly without guile. *Men of yours and my stature.*

The judge had flipped her pencil. Even the registrar had laughed, along with everyone else in the courtroom. Junior lawyer that she was, she had been too focused on the immediate details of the trial to appreciate the large audience that had accumulated behind them throughout the course of two weeks. By 6:00 o'clock that evening, the humiliation of John Jeremey Johnston, Q.C. had become the word on Lawyers' Lane. When she got back to the office that evening, her partners – full of competitive spite – had applauded her.

She had won, what for her was the key issue of the case. That a single father gets to keep his kids, in Toronto, so he can exercise his infrequent access in close proximity. Unheard of, at the time: that a *de minimus* access Dad got to keep a mother from moving. Victory lasted the space of one weekend.

~~~

"Good afternoon, sir."

What she didn't know, as she stood there in the Stratford theatre ticket lineup, is that she would be served with a Notice of Appeal, first thing on the Monday morning – a Notice of Appeal which at that very moment, John Jeremey Johnston Q.C.'s entourage of junior lawyers was drafting.

There would be five appeals on the issue of mobility before the Ontario Court of Appeal, over the ensuing months. The results of each appeal, on different facts, would be that the mother gets to move with the kids. She would report each of these to Al, her client, until the day he would instruct her to concede defeat and allow the appeal, permit the move. He could no longer afford to fight. He was throwing in the towel.

His children would experience their father's conceding the appeal as his abandonment of them.

~~~

Years later, she will bump into one of Al's neighbors, who had been a witness at the trial. The neighbor, according to his own judgment, will tell her what really happened, what became of Cindy and Joe, the bus-driver boyfriend, a fate she might well have predicted. During cross-examination, she had questioned Joe Blanchard about his three failed marriages. From Joe's own mouth, all his marriages turned sour because of his former wives. No admission that bus-driver Joe had played any part in the failure of his three unions. *This* marriage, he'd insisted, would be different. *Cindy was the one. The one he had waited for, all his life.*

"She ran from the house in Thunder Bay to a battered woman's shelter, taking the kids with her, ended up living in a basement apartment. She spent what little was left of her matrimonial settlement from your client. Joe sued Cindy for his entitlement to half of the house in Thunder Bay. They had bought it together with *her* settlement. Marrying Cindy had become his winning lottery ticket. What a loser. Everybody saw it coming. Everybody, but Cindy."

"Why didn't she come back to Toronto?"

"Who knows. Pride? She was determined to make a go of it, in Thunder Bay. Your client Al wasn't much better, not as a parent. No one will talk to him now, least of all his own children. For God's sake, he took up with Cindy's sister in Toronto. She was known to enjoy the odd snort of cocaine. Cindy's sister was the only one who would have him. One of his daughters never spoke to him again, even refused to see him whenever he showed up in Thunder Bay, which was just about never. That kid will dump both parents out of her life, the first chance she gets."

～

"Who was the last person in my room?" she cried in the hospital. "I demand to know who was the last person in my room?"

Hours after her caesarean section, she had run down the hospital corridor to the nursing station. Marco was supposed to be in the room with his mother, but due to the trauma of the birth, he was separated from her, for both their safety. High on medication, she had reasoned that the last person in her room must have *stolen* her baby.

"You are our patient, too," the gentle nurse had said, leading her back to the room, and only then did she realize she had been delusional.

The first time she held Marco in her arms, three days after his birth, she had looked into his face and he had given her a sudden, blessed smile, as if to say, "All will be well, Momma, don't worry, all will be well."

The nurse explained the smile was only gas. The second nurse said, "He is an old soul, a very old soul, a spiritual child." She preferred to believe the second.

She would have walked through fire for this child. She would have done anything. Never would she have abandoned him. She, a mother, who knew herself to be all that stood between her child and the darkness.

~~~

The lights dim. The audience settles. Still brooding about the case, about the silence of her opposing senior counsel, acutely aware of John Jeremy Johnson, Q.C. occupying the same darkness as she, hearing the same words, just as they had listened to the Judge pronouncing judgment, only yesterday. As the curtain falls, and through the next successive acts of the play, she remembers nothing about the play, not its plot, nor its direction, but only what the King says as he anticipates the moment when he will not be able wield a sword, so weary will he be of the fight.

> 'Let me not live,' quoth he,
> 'After my flame lacks oil, to be the snuff
> Of younger spirits...'

In the darkness of the Stratford audience, she wonders how he will be hearing these same words, John Jeremey Johnston, Q.C., her senior counsel by at least three decades, how he will be registering their impact, having just lost to a younger spirit? It is an understanding she cannot have for at least three decades, when it will be her own flame that will lack oil, when she will be the one facing her own darkness. But for now, anyway, she gets to just be in the audience, knowing that tomorrow Marco will come home, without fail.

Jane Callen

GRACE

Epitaph: Everything about Cecily was untimely. Her happenstance creation on the straw-strewn floor of the derelict barn, so soon in her parents' relationship. Her premature arrival two months after their rushed nuptials, when her lungs had not yet learned their ritual. Her death three weeks later, before sunshine warmed her snake-thin arms, or a summer breeze brushed her down-covered scalp, and without ever savouring the soft-bladed sweetness on which she was formed.

"Raindrops keep falling on my head." Arlie belts out her favourite earworm until she runs out of words, then hums what she remembers of the tune. Slamming the metal locker door, she clamps down on the combination lock. It's quarter to three, enough time to grab a coffee in the cafeteria before report and handover. Four days off and it feels like something inside her needs to recalibrate before she can function. How long until the status of registered nurse takes hold, fits her like a layer of skin, not an oversized coat?

Arlie's not crazy about the evening shift. It means she and James barely touch. She climbs into bed exhausted as he crawls out half asleep. Still, it's her favourite shift when it comes to workload. The specialists who expect the nurses to cater to their unreasonable demands and obscure orders are long gone by three o'clock in the afternoon. Only the occasional latecomer shows up for evening rounds. Those doctors are the quiet ones, content to go about their business unaccompanied. They care for their patients without the noise and posturing of department heads who parade through the ward, making a bedside show of drilling the coterie of resident doctors trailing behind them. They revel in publicly uncovering their students' ignorance. Arlie doesn't understand to what end, but she finds them exceptionally unpleasant and shies away from getting in their sights. Nurses can become collateral damage although their practical ward knowledge often exceeds the medical students' theoretical learning.

The evening shift gives Arlie more time to care for her patients, the real nursing work. Once the dinner trays with unappetizing smells are collected, the ward settles down and the focus turns to readying everyone for sleep. Family members drift out without having to be coaxed. There are wounds to dress, backs to massage, and catheters to flush. If she's assigned to the drug cart, a more senior duty, her sole task is to administer the medications on the ward. The job requires her full attention, but interruptions are few and the need to triage her workload is rare. Arlie is thorough. She checks for new orders that may have been missed by the day staff, especially if a physician conducted late rounds. Accurate dosing is critical. She double-checks the cart and insists on reading their identification bracelets even when she knows the patient by name. Once the meds are distributed, she observes for untoward side effects. That aging diabetic in 10B still isn't stable and plunges into hypoglycemic sweats too often. She'll keep watch over him all evening. Having finished her charting, Arlie savours the satisfaction that comes from a job well executed.

She trained in a teaching hospital, but its school of nursing has since closed. Now student nurses attend a university or community college. Hers was an apprenticeship on the front lines of the busiest hospital in Montreal, The Royal Victoria. Although she graduated less than twelve months ago, Arlie was already considered to be what they call "old school" in her approach to patient care. It means she understands there's an art as well as a science to nursing, having witnessed both first-hand. Book-trained nurses can quote the science, but they don't have the feel for the work that three years of ward experience brings. At least, that's what Arlie thinks.

The rest of the nursing team's already in the staff room when Arlie arrives on Johnson 3 Medical, but she's not technically late because they're waiting for Peanut. That's the awful moniker the Chief of Medicine uses to address their Head Nurse. Peanut's on the phone with her Director, which doesn't bode well and probably means last-minute staff changes. A quick head count reveals there are four registered and two practical nurses to manage the forty-bed medical unit tonight. Arlie settles in beside the assistant head who is writing a grocery list on the back of an envelope stamped with the hospital logo. They wait.

Finally off the phone, Peanut tells her team about staffing changes, as Arlie had guessed. They're short on Brock 6 Surgery, Peanut says, so we need to send a float from our ward. Reorganizing their assignments, she assigns her most senior staff to double duty – meds and acting head nurse. The acting head nurse will administer the medications while managing whatever unexpected medical events arise during the evening. That's a heavy load, and Arlie's glad she's too junior to have it thrust upon her. The buck-toothed RN gets the north side of the ward, and the newcomer from Quebec City, whose name Arlie forgets, is assigned to the south side. Peanut shunts Arlie off to Brock 6 Surgical.

"Take a practical nurse with you because they're full up with fresh post-ops."

Cheryl volunteers. She's the quiet PN with skin still bronzed from her Caribbean honeymoon. Arlie's glad for the backup because the PN knows Brock 6. Arlie's never worked there. Besides, she dreads the unexpected urgencies that can arise with fresh post-ops. Cheryl will know what to do if she doesn't.

"Wait," Peanut addresses Arlie and the PN. "I've an announcement to make before you head over to 6." Peanut, who barely reaches five feet, makes an effort to stand tall. She scans her team. "Rachel Nelles is on Sydenham 7. She was admitted last evening. Attempted suicide."

Arlie feels the oxygen suck out of the room, has trouble getting a breath. The nurses look from one to the other, trying to absorb this news. Rachel is the PN who recently returned from Mat leave after her preemie baby died last month. Now she tried to kill herself.

"She'll recover..." Peanut sits down, and pulls her clipboard onto her lap. "Eventually." Thinking that Peanut's announcement was over, Arlie rises and nods to Cheryl that they should leave. The assistant head nurse stops making her shopping list and asks the question they all want answered. "How?"

"OD of chloral hydrate," the most common sleep remedy on the drug cart.

Arlie checks the others, but perceives no reactions. She is sick with fear for what she might hear next.

"It wasn't prescribed. She apparently got it from the nurses she works with." Peanut stares at her team, tapping the clipboard with her pen again and again.

How many of those orange bullets does it take to overdose? Arlie wants to escape, needs to collect the thoughts whirling about her brain. But Peanut continues.

"She won't say who gave her the pills, only that no one gave her more than one dose at a time. No one knew what she planned to do."

Arlie's hand is glued to the door of the nurse's office. Just turn the knob and go. You're late for handover on 6. Then Peanut answers Arlie's unspoken question.

"At 500 mg each, a conservative estimate is that it would take eight to ten capsules, possibly more, to do the job. That means that some of you, or all of you, gave her the drug." The room is thick with silence, except for the tapping of Peanut's pen. "I don't know what we can do about it…giving a dose of uncontrolled sedative to someone for sleep isn't a crime any more than if you'd given her a Tylenol for a headache, but…"

Peanut surveys her staff, peers into each face. Arlie feels naked as Peanut's eyes meet her own, but she wills herself not to blink. "Mother Elizabeth must conduct an investigation. Even she isn't certain what that means. We've never dealt with something like this before." The dense silence that follows is cut by Peanut's exhausted sigh.

She puts down her pen, picks up her clipboard, and switches gears. "Report. Who's first?" A nod to Arlie. "The two of you need to go. You're already late for 6."

The nurses on Brock 6 have already dispersed to work the ward when Arlie and Cheryl arrive. At the nurses station, a middle-aged woman gives them the once over.

"You sure took your time, ladies. Report is over." She surveys the charts spread across the desk in front of her, then directs Cheryl to find the nurse working the west side of the ward. "Do whatever she needs to help out. She's got a heavy load." Arlie watches her recede down the corridor.

"Follow me." The nurse strides down the hall to the opposite end of the ward, stops outside a private room with the cautionary ISOLATION on the door. "Fresh post-op, bowel resection. He's septic," she mouths her words, rather than saying them. "Probably won't make it through the night."

The patient is sealed away in this isolation room here, not in the Intensive Care Unit, so that his infection will not spread to other patients there. Gowned, capped and gloved for her own protection, Arlie surveys her patient – a thirty-eight-year-old male with a tear in his gut – who did not seek medical help until

Jane Callen

yesterday, despite days of excruciating pain. He developed sep-
ticemia as bacteria spread throughout his body. The offending
length of colon was resected, his system flushed clean, and
masses of antibiotics now stream through his veins. Only three
hours post-op and already he's showing signs of organ failure.

Arlie's role tonight is that of watcher – the keeper of vital signs
that she must measure and record every thirty minutes. Blood
pressure, temperature, pulse, respirations, urine output, level of
consciousness, pupil dilation, colour. She monitors the flow of
fluids through his two cut-down intravenous lines, one stitched
into his arm and the other into his leg. Calls for replenishments
when the cocktail of drugs in the IV bags get low. If anything
changes, she's to alert the nurses' station. Unless he crashes, then
she's to call a Code Blue to summon the resuscitation cart and
emergency responders.

Her semi-conscious patient groans when he is touched. His
metrics remain unchanged. He's still close to flat-lining, as the
head nurse warned. Arlie is halfway through the evening shift.
Soon someone will come relieve her for the dinner break. If he's
going to die, she wants to be in the cafeteria when it happens.
Beyond recording his measurements, there's not much Arlie can
do for him. She stares out the window onto Brock Street as the
daylight fades. Traffic lightens and the sidewalk empties of
passersby. She glances back at her patient, scans him for changes.
Finds none. This aspect of nursing Arlie finds daunting: how to
feel at ease in her skin as she deals with life and death, when there's
no certainty or pattern to rely on.

Broad bands of white cotton bind Rachel's wrists securing them
to the bedrails with a professional knot that Arlie is certain she
couldn't replicate. Sensing a presence, the body belonging to the
tethered hands turns. A tumble of black hair spills over the coarse
woollen blanket. Rachel's looks could be described as startling in

their beauty. Despite surviving a suicide attempt and the manual flush of toxins from her body, her complexion is a vibrant blush of peach.

"Arlie, you came." The smile she attempts reveals an elegant row of teeth, but the strain in her voice betrays her ordeal.

Arlie inches closer, presses her sternum against the bedrail, and places her palm on a captive arm. Feeling Rachel's warmth, Arlie shivers. She thinks they'd put her in a white coffin just like her dead baby.

Misreading the shiver, "I'm not saying who gave me the pills." Her dark eyes fix on Arlie. "Everyone needs to know that. Tell them." Spent from delivering her message, she turns away. "This was my plan, mine alone."

"I wished I'd known how bad things were. Perhaps I could've gotten you some help." Arlie strokes her tethered forearm, fighting an impulse to set Rachel free.

"I've enough help, thanks." She turns back to face Arlie with a thin smile and a futile attempt to raise her fist. "I knew we were finished when Russ packed up Cicely's tiny cotton nighties, even the sweater I knitted to bring her home. It was melon coloured 'cause we didn't know if she was a girl or a boy." Tears leak through thick lashes. Rachel squeezes her eyes shut as if to stop them. "We married because I got knocked up, so…" Using her feet for leverage she inches higher in the bed, struggles to find a comfortable position. On her back she resembles a prisoner more than a patient. "He said we needed to do the honourable thing."

"Can I get you something? Are you in pain?" Arlie knows there's nothing she can do to give Rachel relief.

"Untie me. Just give me a few minutes." Rachel's eyes open wide. Arlie feels a gut wrench, similar to the one that accompanied Rachel's initial request – *Just one capsule, I can't seem to sleep anymore.*

They're in a private room at the junction joining the south and north wings of Sydenham 7. It's the room where the nursing sisters stay when they're hospitalized because it's removed from the noise of daily foot traffic. Chances are she could loosen Rachel's tethers and not be found out. Except that's what she thought the last time too. And look what happened.

"I'm sorry, I can't." Knowing this isn't good enough. "I'll call the nurse in charge. I'm sure she could authorize removing them for a while."

"Don't bother. They always say no." Defeated, Rachel's voice slips away. Arlie realizes she's medicated. At least these are pre-scribed drugs this time. "He said there was no good reason to stay now that Cecily was gone. No need to be honourable anymore, I guess. So Russ packed up his guitar and walked away."

Arlie leans over the bedrail because Rachel's words are so gar-bled, almost impossible to make out.

"Time for me to go too. I wanted to be with Cecily...I still do." She underlines her words with a fierceness unfamiliar to Arlie. "But he came back because he forgot his fucking guitar stand, and so he found me."

Rachel drifts away under the influence of the prescribed meds. Anti-anxiety, she guesses. Arlie watches, lost in Rachel's words, in what it must have felt like to lose your baby and then have your man walk away. Unaware when Mother Elizabeth enters the room, she startles when the nun joins her at the bedrail.

"She asked to have the restraints released."

"I know," says Mother Elizabeth, patting the silver crucifix resting on her ample chest. "Rachel hasn't decided whether she wants to stay with us or join her baby. Until we believe that she's decided to stay, the restraints remain."

The last act Arlie performs for the patient in 12A is to tie a name tag to the great toe of her right foot with a piece of string. She's been bathed, the multiple tubes that supported her life after the massive stroke have been removed and placed in a plastic bag for disposal. Pulling the white plastic sheet over the cadaver, Arlie dials up the morgue from the bedside table, alerts them that their patient is ready for transport.

"Yours or ours?" Mother Elizabeth or one of her staff reports always asks whenever Arlie calls in a death. She didn't give much thought to the fact that the hospital was run by a Catholic order when she accepted their offer of employment. She was more interested in the fact that she'd found work in Kingston where James had been recently posted. She expected the crucifixes on the walls and understood that the nuns would oversee her work, but she didn't chase down what that might mean on a practical level. Raised by fervent Fundamental Baptists, she'd had her fill of religious restrictions from an early age. Arlie ignores the topic of God, believing in only what she can see and touch.

Yours or ours. If the patient states they are Catholic on admission, the Holy Sisters of St. Joseph guide their journey after death. A sister, or if the status of the dead is worthy, Mother Elizabeth herself supervises the preparation of the body, assures that Last Rites are performed by the Reverend Father, and accompanies the grieving kin when they pay their respects. As the body's lifted onto a gurney with the false top that hides the transport of the dead from casual onlookers in the hospital corridors, Mother Elizabeth guides the living to her private quarters for tea and open-faced sandwiches. As the morgue staff slide the corpse onto a shelf in the refrigeration unit, the Reverend Mother prays a liturgy dedicated to the occasion. If warranted by their parish standing, a priest joins her. This is the care that Catholic patients receive on their demise.

However, if the patient identifies as Protestant, another faith, agnostic, or simply declines to disclose a faith category, that individual falls into the hands of Arlie and her fellow non-Catholics.

Death via the express route is functional and without ceremony. The body is washed and bagged. The gurney arrives, and the dead are dispatched to the morgue. Next of kin are given a few minutes with their deceased on the ward if they're quick about it. Otherwise, they're left to make their own arrangements with the morgue or funeral home.

The patient in 12A was hers, not theirs. She was also her last duty of the day. Pulling on her bell-bottoms and the azure tie-dyed tee, she remembers last summer's rain at Woodstock and James carrying her piggyback across the field when she lost her sandal in the mud. Arlie clangs the door of her locker shut. Sometimes it sticks if she doesn't use enough force. Three-thirty. Time enough to visit Rachel before heading out to meet James for supper in the cafeteria.

The corridors to the north and south wings of Sydenham 7 are empty. The day team huddles in the nursing office giving report and handover to the evening staff. Three days since Rachel was admitted, two since Arlie last saw her. She hopes those damn restraints are gone, that things have improved. She's not even certain what progress might look like in this situation. Preparing herself for whatever lies beyond, she opens the oak-veneer door.

What she finds is an unoccupied bed, an empty room. Her breathing shallows. Have they transferred Rachel to the psych hospital, that madhouse across town next to the prison? She searches the bedside table drawer for signs of an inhabitant. A Mason Pearson hairbrush with tangles of black hair. A cherry-flavoured ChapStick. And the ubiquitous Gideon Bible. Good, she's still here. Her conclusion is confirmed by shuffling feet at the doorway. Lost in a bundle of candy-pink chenille and matching fuzzy slip-ons, Rachel scuffs her way into the room accompanied by a blonde nurse who guides her to the Naugahyde armchair.

Rachel lands with a bulky pink plop. Arlie recognizes the nurse from cafeteria lines.

"You work on Johnson 3 Medical, don't you?" Although Arlie's in street clothes, the nurse recognizes her and shoots her a withering stare. "The ward where Rachel managed to get the unauthorized sedatives from staff." The judgment in her voice, clear.

Powerless out of uniform and on unfamiliar terrain, Arlie fixes her gaze on Rachel and ignores the nurse's insinuation. "How are you feeling, Rae?" Pulling an armless chair closer, she settles in front of Rachel with her back to the inquisitor.

Getting the message, the nurse edges towards the door. "I'll be back in half an hour with your *prescribed* medication." The door taps shut behind her.

"You're feeling better?" Arlie leans in, takes Rachel's previously bound hands into her own. The heat of her flesh warms Arlie's cool palms. "The restraints are gone."

"They've drugged me instead. Imipramine and Lorazepam." Her speech is slowed by lips that struggle to form words. The dark eyes fight to hold Arlie's, to stay open. Psychiatry's answer to patient management.

"Are you receiving any other treatment?' Arlie holds her breath. Please, not ECT. As a student, she accompanied patients to electric convulsive therapy. She witnessed them bound to the gurney, a padded tongue depressor thrust between their lips, their backs arching as electricity shot through their sedated torsos. Then the purple protruding tongues, the unseeing stares. Afterwards, their dazed state was not much different than how Rachel appears now, but it was deemed a positive result.

Rachel shakes her head, pushes a hank of black hair out of her eyes. "They just talk. Talk, talk, talk. Dr. Lanzio talks about making plans for the future. Mother Elizabeth talks about Cecily being in Christ's arms like He's her new babysitter. Father Thomas, poor old man, doesn't know what to say. So he just pats my head and prays the rosary." A failed attempt at a laugh morphs into a snort. "They can't do it." She grasps Arlie's arm, her fingers press down. "They can't talk Cecily away." A tear slips down her cheek, followed by others. A candy pink chenille forearm fails to wipe them away. "Nor can they make me stay." Even with pharmaceutical restraints, Rae's choice remains unchanged.

Having charted that despite the application of butterfly tapes there's continued dehiscence of the abdominal wound of the patient in 14A, Arlie closes the metal folder and returns the file to its slot on the carrousel. She adjusts the bobby pins holding her cap in place as she enters the nurses' office. Being the last one in the crowded glass cube, Arlie's out of luck. Nowhere to sit. She leans against the counter instead. She may be twenty-two, but she's exhausted and her calves ache. She takes turns standing on tiptoe, left foot, and then right. Gets some relief.

It's been a punishing day. She has three new admissions to work up, and two patients with chronic abscesses require sterile flushes and redressing. She can still smell the sickly stench from those wounds. Let's not forget the dementia case who keeps trying to escape; her Johnny-shirt billowing behind her as she runs barefoot for the elevator. Arlie wants to see the end of this shift, peel off her uniform, and head home to three days off, two of them with James.

They're halfway through handover and Arlie's turn is next. She pulls notes from her pocket, reminding herself to mention the abdominal suture line that continues to open. A rap on the door interrupts her debrief. Heads turn. There's Rachel dressed in an over-sized purple sweater and Black Watch tartan slacks, accompanied by a woman who looks remarkably like her. After a moment of surprise, the nurses surround and embrace their own. Arlie joins in, wrapping her arms around the others. Rachel is hidden somewhere in the middle.

Murmurs of conversation overlap. Rae, how are you doing? Ah, sweetie! And *Je suis désolée* from Martine, the new arrival from Quebec City. Arlie looks up, catches Peanut surveying her team. Her mouth lost to a thin, tight line, she meets Arlie's gaze and gives a barely perceptible nod. And Arlie knows, even Peanut.

We all did it! Sisters of Mercy, they call us. Nurses who pledge to abstain from whatever is deleterious, to not knowingly administer any harmful drug. We took the Nightingale Pledge at graduation, and we gave Rachel the orange gel caps. We knew it was medication for patients, not for our own use. But we also knew that chloral hydrate is a stock medication, ordered in bulk from the pharmacy. It wasn't someone's prescription that would be meted out, dose by dose. Counted. Ignoring hospital rules and our professional ethics, one by one we gave in to Rachel's request because we didn't think we'd get caught. We gave her enough poison to end her life. If Russ hadn't returned to the house, we'd all be accomplices to Rachel's death. This is what Arlie wants to scream.

The coven loosens its grip. Rachel emerges and pushes her unwashed hair out of her eyes. Handover report forgotten, they listen as she explains she's going home. The woman beside her, her sister, is staying with her for the time being. But Rachel hopes to return to work. Her voice falters and she shrugs. Arlie knows that making plans to return to work is beyond the scope of the meds that pollute Rachel's veins. Still, those chemical restraints are doing their job. They're keeping Rachel here against her will.

Call bells sound at the nursing station. Rachel takes her leave with a promise to drop by whenever she's downtown. Arlie gives the Coles Notes version of her report. She's free to go, but the dementia patient is on the loose again, escaping unknown terrors. Arlie won't leave yet. She's figured out the route the demented woman travels and offers to help the evening nurse round her up.

Martine joins Arlie in the alcove where unused wheelchairs are stored, just before the double doors that separate the ward from the elevators.

"She runs from doorway to doorway along the length of the ward," Arlie explains the patient's pattern. "She's like an urban commando."

"I wonder what she fears is lurking, waiting for her?"

"Us, I suppose." Laughter. The kind that bonds in uneasy circumstances.

A glimpse of blue Johnny-shirt and a high-pitched wail alert them to the patient's location down the corridor. She's about halfway.

"We could have killed her." Arlie fixes her eyes on the hallway.

"None of us wanted that," Martine places her hand on Arlie's shoulder. "I look at it another way. She lied, betrayed our trust. If she'd managed to die, think of the damage to those who only wished to give her comfort." Martine gives Arlie a quick embrace. "We were saved from such a tragedy. I think each of us, we received God's grace."

With a rush of blue and a tinny screech, the demented woman dashes towards them. Her knees held high, her bare feet slap flat-footed as they hit the linoleum. The nurses wait until she's almost to the swinging doors. When the Johnny-shirt is close enough to touch, Arlie steps in front of the patient and hooks her arm around the wasted torso. Martine rolls a wheelchair up to the boney rump, which flashes from beneath the hospital nightie. Together they manoeuvre the woman into the chair. It's not difficult. She's emaciated and lacks the cognitive ability to fight back. The ambush stops her keening. Sniffing the air, she attempts to ascertain what's happening.

"You're safe, Madame. I'm here to help you," Martine coos over and over as she wheels her captive down the corridor. The woman in the wheelchair cocks her head. Tries to locate the sound. Arlie monitors their progress until Martine arrives at the dementia patient's room, then she pushes her way through the double doors leading outside. Three days off and two of them with James.

Yakos Spiliotopoulos

GRAVE DIGGER

In the spring of 1948, during some of the darkest days of the Civil War, six soldiers from the Greek army were executed by partisans at the side of the road outside our village. None of the dead were locals. Nobody knew much about them at all. But our community had to take care of the bodies.

It wasn't as simple as calling army people, or even the families. There were no phones. Even if there were, it would have taken weeks to get an army carriage out to our remote Aroania mountain village, if it wasn't ambushed. The only solution was to bury them in our cemetery.

They asked me to dig the graves. It wasn't an unusual request. I was fourteen then, and strong, and my family needed the money. They told me to dig the holes next to the cypress tree in the far corner of the cemetery, away from any of the other graves – almost in Barba Yianni's fields. The muddy soil stuck to my bare feet as I dug throughout that drizzly day. Father Dimitri was with me, sitting down and quietly smoking cigarettes under a chestnut tree, watching me work. He was a good priest. He married my parents, and baptized me and my four brothers. It was sad when I dug his grave only a year later.

Just as I finished, a tall, thick, unshaven military man arrived on a horse. Following behind him were two soldiers, skinny, and not much older than I, driving the church's horse-drawn carriage loaded with coffins. The unshaven man, obviously their commander, dismounted and barked out orders at the two soldiers, who hurriedly carried the caskets and placed them in their holes.

"Open the caskets," Father Dimitri said to the commander.

"Just get on with it," the commander shouted. There were dark lines under his eyes. "The bodies are in bad shape."

"These boys didn't get a proper Orthodox funeral. No families crying for them, no friends. I want their caskets open."

The commander glared at Father Dimitri, then snapped his fingers in the direction of the two soldiers. They quickly jumped into the holes and opened each casket, wincing as they did. One of them threw up. I almost did as well. All the bodies gave off a putrid stench. Three of the dead had been shot in the head, leaving their faces mangled and unrecognizable. The other ones seemed to be sizzling with decomposition. All of them somehow felt more dead than the many other bodies I had buried.

The soldiers struggled back out, helping each other, and stood at attention. Father Dimitri said prayers for the six men, unfazed, even as the rain poured down harder and harder. I watched as drops of water drenched his long grey beard. When he finished, the soldiers climbed down and quickly closed the caskets.

"These boys are just teenagers," Father Dimitri said to the commander, shaking his head. "Do their mothers know what happened?"

"We'll send word to the families," he replied, then waived me forward. I moved the soil as fast as I could over the six caskets while the soldiers tied wooden crosses together and drove them into the ground at the heads. When we finished, I stood with Father Dimitri while the commanding officer spoke with the two soldiers. There was some sort of confusion. The commander was angry.

"You didn't keep track of where you put them?" the commander shouted, standing very close to the soldiers. "These boys gave their lives for us and we can't even mark their graves right?"

The soldiers trembled and looked down. The commander turned his hard stare to me, and to the graves. He suddenly flung the two soldiers to the ground and pushed their faces into the mud.

"If I had more men available," he screamed, "I'd have you two digging these graves with your bare hands."

He held their faces down. They were writhing, struggling to breathe.

"Enough!" shouted Father Dimitri.

The commander let go. The soldiers gasped on the ground. He spat at them, then ordered them up and into the carriage. They pulled away, not saying goodbye. Father Dimitri and I were left standing in the rain.

Three years later, I met Andreas at our village bazaar. I had heard all about Andreas driving a pick-up truck even before I met him. Nobody in our village owned a car back then. He had been to see the mayor and the police – some were saying he worked for the king himself.

From where I was selling walnuts, I watched Andreas enter the bazaar. He was tall and fair-skinned, almost pale. He spoke with Penelope – she sold teas near the entrance – and she pointed at me. The stranger approached.

"Are you Nikos?" he asked.

I nodded nervously.

"My name is Andreas. I've come from Kerkira to find my brother Spiros. He was in the national army and was killed three years ago with five others around here. I heard you buried them."

"I dug the graves," I said.

"Can you tell me which one of those graves is my brother?" he asked. He handed me a black-and-white photo of a curly haired soldier proudly saluting.

"I can't remember," I said, returning the photo.

"Are you sure?" he said, pushing the photo back. "The mayor, the police – nobody's helping me."

That wasn't surprising. I may have been just a boy back then, but I knew how everything worked. The wounds from the Civil War were still fresh, and our village was divided.

"My mother cries every day," Andreas said, taking the picture. "My father can't sleep. We sold half our flocks just to hire the truck. All I want is to bring him home."

I knew that many in the bazaar were watching us. I wanted to tell Andreas I couldn't help, so I wouldn't arouse suspicion or rumours. But when I looked at his eyes all I could see was my mother, just a few years earlier, when she got the letter that my father wasn't coming home from the war. That his body hadn't been recovered.

"I'll help," I said.

Just after midnight we met at the cemetery. I brought two shovels, and he brought the oil lamp, like we planned. We started digging as quietly as we could, not lighting the lamp in case we were noticed. The half moon was bright, giving us all the light we needed. Every few minutes we silenced one another, thinking we had heard someone coming. Each time it was nothing.

I hit the first grave. We quickly removed the soil until we revealed the entire wooden box. We opened it, covering our faces with rags from the terrible smell, and lit the lamp. There were maggots and bugs everywhere, crawling through the mouth, even the eye sockets. I could hardly look.

"I'm not sure," Andreas said.

We continued until we hit another grave. We opened it like the first.

"This is Spiros," Andreas said right away, holding the lamp with one hand and a rag over his face with the other.

"How do you know?"

"The hair."

The body was almost a complete skeleton, and there was a big hole in the forehead, but for some reason the hair was still there. Blonde and curly, like Andreas'.

"I'll help dig the others to be sure," I said.

Andreas didn't respond. He just stared at the corpse.

"This is Spiros," he said after a time, wiping a tear from his face.

I didn't question him. We lifted the grave out and put it in the back of the truck, then replaced the soil over the holes. When we finally finished, Andreas reached into his pocket and removed a handful of bills.

"No," I said.

"Take it," he said.

I pushed his hand away. He thanked me and drove off, his lights bright on the horizon.

I enter the cemetery through the rusted gates and push aside weeds with my cane as I make my way along the narrow path to Elena's *mnima*. I open the glass chamber at the head of the marble encasement, put a small bag of *koliva* next to her photo, and sit down on the edge.

Elena was buried here three years ago. It has been hard. The priest mentioned her today in church, but that's the most people do now. Nobody misses her like I do. Even our kids rushed off, back to Patras with their own families, after the service this morning.

No matter. I'm happier alone, and it's peaceful out here. The old cypress tree next to Elena squeaks as it sways in the wind, like an old fence door fluttering open and closed. On the other side of the tree, in this crowded corner of the cemetery, are the graves of those soldiers I buried. The wooden crosses all lie on the ground now, rotting where they once stood. I think of Andreas. He sent me a few letters afterward, mostly saying thanks, and telling me his brother was given a proper burial. He also spoke of going to Australia, or maybe even America, for work. After that the letters stopped.

There's talk now of digging the soldiers' graves up to make room in the cemetery. I chuckle, thinking about the wild explanations that would emerge in the village about the missing casket. I would surely be asked about it, but I'll never tell anyone what happened. Elena was the only person I ever told, and that story will stay in this ground forever when I'm buried with her one day.

Chris Urquhart

SKINBOUND

Daphne started to sweat when her skin grew algae and green buds burst from her pores. At first these spots resembled warts, then oddly shaped burns. Soon her skin paled, curled, rippled, and grew. She started becoming something she had never seen before.

"Your cells aren't the problem, but the spaces between them are sick," Dr. Hink said, spreading his knowledgeable hands across her now-budding chest. Chester Hink, a renowned dermatologist, specialized in infectious diseases. "I developed the method to balance your cells back to normal again, cupcake. My team can save your body. And it's not *algae*. It's called *cyanobacteria*."

"Have you ever seen this before, Doctor?" Her breath was now fast and shallow.

"Never," Dr. Hink told her, "*especially* not in a woman."

Their eyes met for an instant, then both stared downward, wordlessly, as Dr. Hink grabbed his tools and began the job of cutting into her. Daphne listened to the whir and buzz of the doctor's saw as pieces of herself fell to the floor.

The first marks had sprung up on her right thigh. She'd nicked herself with a steak knife over Sunday dinner (they'd been eating strip loin). It was a millisecond oversight, really. She'd felt it the moment it happened – the violation, her stupid mistake – but she'd kept quiet. She'd also stained her mother's new tablecloth in the process. She'd felt it, at least she thought she had felt it – the alien entry, the pulsing, new feeling crawling up inside her circulatory system – but she could have never imagined that this tiny flesh wound could eventually turn her into something entirely different.

The nurses came back in when excision was complete, avoiding eye contact. They picked up Daphne's heavy, leafy body and transferred it efficiently from operating table to gurney. Some wore arm-length plastic gloves for touching her. Others even held their breath, which Daphne found particularly rude. She was able to walk, but she let the nurses do their job. The nurses pushed her through many doors and dank hallways until they reached a brightly lit, private hospital room with a washroom at one end with a tub and sink. Two adjustable beds, pushed together and both in the lowest position, occupied the other end.

Are these both for me? How big have I actually grown?

∽

"You're overreacting," Daphne's mother informed her on the phone that evening. "It sounds more like the skin infection Uncle Carl had last spring."

"Mom, I have roots coming out of my crotch."

"Oh, Daphne, please. Anyway, you say it's some kind of HPV virus that caused this infection? That's the wacko doctor's theory? Is that a Sexually Transmitted Disease, honey? Be honest with me."

"I— I'm not sure. And it's Sexually Transmitted Infection now, Mom."

"Well, you haven't got a new boyfriend have you, Daphne?" Daphne had not had a boyfriend since she was 12 years old – a fact her mother made a concerted effort to ignore. "If so, bring him to the barbecue on Sunday. The more, the merrier. Honey, does he eat fish or steak? Or is he another one of those horrible vegans?"

"Never mind," Daphne mumbled into the receiver, which now emitted a dull beep. She slurred an excuse to her mother and hung up. Where her navel used to indent it was now black and encrusted, twenty times the size of her old innie belly button, and hardening quickly. It turned and swelled as she watched herself changing, transfixed.

Dr. Hink had said she'd be here in hospital a week. Two at tops. They would continue shearing therapy, the nurses would take a few more rounds of stool and blood samples, run tests, and provide medication at no cost to Daphne, due to the experimental nature of this study

No one had seen anything like Daphne before. Treatment was voluntary, she reminded herself. She'd signed the waiver and disclaimer forms without worry, as long as they could fix this issue, and quickly. She knew she needed to be monitored – for her own safety and for that of the public.

From the other room, the TV blared and buzzed in the background.

"Today on Maury: Teen tells mother he's in love with a...TREE-HUGGER!"

Daphne removed her tightening hospital gown and crawled into the hospital tub with difficulty. She plugged the drain and turned the water to full heat. Daphne squatted, longing to take refuge underwater. She grasped her pink razor in her (now sprouting) palm: Daphne shaved through arm-length green leafy growth and knobby bits of bark. Her pink razor bumped up against her new outsides. Daphne longed to control her situation, to harvest herself back into some kind of female form, but her efforts were futile. The green was winning. She couldn't recognize her skin beyond bark at most parts. Unable to submerge herself completely, she gave up and pulled the plug.

∽

Daphne's cousin Harold, Uncle Carl's son, had blown off his middle finger in an explosives accident in Northern Alberta, where he drove trucks for highway demolition. When Harold showed up one finger less last year to the family barbeque, everyone acted like everything was normal. Carl and Harold cracked jokes and beers as usual. Nobody said anything. Daphne wondered how her family would understand her now. Growths were much different than voids. Subtraction was safe, but you had to make sense of extras.

∽

Dr. Hink's lab smelled like raw hot dogs. Daphne felt immediately sick upon noticing the stench when she entered. "You've grown again, cupcake!" the doctor informed her, after pulling open her medical gown.

Hink was right: She had grown an inch or two upwards and outwards every hour. The treatments were not working. In fact, things seemed to be getting much worse. Full branches had begun to form around her neck and lower back, and their girth was thickening.

Dr. Hink instructed her to slide under a cold machine, which zipped to-and-fro above her body. She hyperventilated for many minutes, and tried to tell herself to calm down.

Dr. Hink watched and talked to her through headphones from another room outside the lab. "Don't move, Daphne."

Didn't he understand? I am growing, not moving.

After many more minutes Dr. Hink returned, a bit hesitant but oddly excited. "I know this is going to sound strange, Daphne, but, well, it seems that your bones are, well, *disappearing.*"

"What do you mean?"

"Well, you're becoming a sort of human tree – bone free, with a rough bark-like exterior. White skin, shoots, and now full branches bearing green foliage. Your bones are slowly fading from our scans, somehow; it's really most astounding! As much as I can estimate from your exterior presentation, you resemble a *Betula pendula*, or silver birch, as it is more commonly known here."

Dr. Hink noticed she was upset only when tears rolled down her cheeks. "Look, at least you're not one of those awful black poplars or Japanese maples," he attempted, but her distress only worsened. Daphne was upset, uncomfortable in the gown, and having a hard time concentrating on the information she was receiving. She was distracted by an audience ooing and awing from a blaring TV, but she wasn't sure where it came from. Daphne focussed back in on her doctor, who had continued speaking without pause.

"Don't worry, Daphne, these advanced treatments will work. I know it's hard for you to grasp right now. Please, just lie there. Try to relax."

∽

The next day Daphne explained to Dr. Hink that she needed a day-pass to see her family for a "religious holiday." But when he refused, she made a calculated escape after breakfast. She drove north to the family barbecue, limbs and branches stuffed in the back seat of her truck. She saw the roadside trees, green and gold, reflected in her windshield rearview mirror. Every ounce of her ached. She reached the park turnoff and stopped at the roadside. It was only a short walk to the family barbecue from here. Daphne lugged herself from the pickup and slammed the door behind her.

She was suddenly confronted with a deep, foreign calmness. She walked slowly into the bush across the wet and prickly forest floor. Light fell through branches. She ventured further, found an open spot, and lay down. Daphne saw a small, decaying fly-covered carcass next to her. She examined the mammal's small frame – pale, collapsed – still covered in bits of hair and rot. She knew that no matter how many times those bones broke, small pieces would become buried underground like tired bits of biology.

Daphne considered all the evolutionary features humans once owned – gills, fins, non-opposable thumbs, tails for some). Vines and tendrils creep around her earlobes, sneaking silently into eardrums and down her canals. The smell of steak and hot dogs wafted past her, barely noticed. Daphne could no longer hear. Instead of panic, she felt peace.

Sunlight fed her form. She became spineless, boneless, skinless. To some, she may have looked like a fallen woman – a timbered tree – splayed helplessly on the forest floor. Daphne looked upwards under the swelling sun, not bound by roots, blood, or bones.

Norman Snider

HUSBAND MATERIAL

Olivia Keller, after a bad divorce, has developed strict rules about men. Curtis, her blue-eyed ex, played guitar in bars all over the country and was never home. And she knew from harsh experience what happens with guitar players and women in bars.

Exuding alcohol fumes, blonde Curtis looms flat-stomached over the tub where the two children bathe, haloed by alcohol fumes. He ignores her protests as he immerses himself fully clothed into the water. The children are uncertain how to respond. He's been gone a solid month. Olivia had met him in a club where he was dazzling the customers. Young Galahad with a hot rod customized Fender Telecaster. For two years they couldn't get enough of each other. Curtis sees himself as a reckless adventurous free spirit, unfettered by the bonds of a clone-like humanity enslaved by trivia. Away in Tulsa or Seattle, swept away in a flood of addictions, he seldom phones home. Olivia looks on as he splashes around, trying to decide which girlfriend to tell this story to first. She recognizes that the bath time episode with Curtis is motivated by disappointment – chagrin that he's still playing bars and not arenas and concert halls, that he'll never be more than a sideman.

So, no more musicians. Ditto actors and pro athletes. They were, to a man, vain, selfish, love 'em and leave 'em types, out for themselves. She has Nicholas and Emily, her wonderful kids, And, taking it easy on the white wine, at 35 she still keeps a pretty good figure. Olivia knows when she sashays into a room, with her lovely smile and ballerina's demure hips, she still attracts the attention of men.

Kevin H. Book, for instance. Two or three years younger than Olivia, he works in sales at Frames, the film and television distribution company where she runs the IT department. Olivia thinks bland Kevin doesn't look like much. Definitely not Curtis' equal for looks. With thinning oatmeal hair, the bespectacled face of a YMCA instructor in 1919, and big white front teeth. The only thing missing is the high, celluloid collar. But everybody in the firm likes his reliability.

Today, Olivia runs into Kevin at coffee break in the employee's kitchen on the second floor. He's always talking about his two kids, so that gives them a topic of conversation. Olivia believes she has learned how to communicate clearly and without ambivalence. It's part of her job. Kevin is so good with those kids, she thinks. He's such a devoted father. They talk about Halloween and he tells her how he built an entire display in the front of his Mississauga house with spiderwebs and witches on brooms. Kevin had found a job in a publisher's shipping room out of high school, moved on to sales rep, and was now selling to film exhibitors instead of bookstores. You'd think his wife would appreciate him more. He does everything around that house, including the cooking. Olivia knows Kevin has trouble at home; she is happy that he trusts her sufficiently to confide in her. Apparently, Kevin, poor guy, took his two boys out trick-or-treating while Rebecca, the wife, went to a dinner party with some of her friends in advertising. And she didn't come back until two in the morning.

You can't let her get away with stuff like that, says a smiling Olivia.

I know, says Kevin, but you don't know her. You don't know what she's like when she gets mad.

You shouldn't let her take advantage. Stand up for yourself! Kevin's weak, Olivia thinks. No false machismo with this dude.

Kevin smiles back at her shyly. He'll try to be more assertive at home.

In the ladies' washroom that afternoon, Olivia thoroughly investigates the topic of Kevin and his marriage with her best friend, Lily Chen, personal assistant to Denton Frame, their hot-head boss.

Poor Kevin is so patient with that wife of his, says Olivia.

She sounds awful. Lily's from Hong Kong, tiny as a sparrow. She's a serious woman, just like her friend Olivia. Maybe a little too schoolteacher serious, in her rimless specs. She and Olivia visit polite living rooms together, take cooking classes, and attend the ballet.

Absolutely, says Olivia.

Lily then goes on to relate her most recent disastrous date, a divorced dentist she met through an online dating site. She says the conversation needed two Nubians to carry it. That's her favourite description of an evening with a new guy where the talk lags in an embarrassing way. Great silent gaps. Olivia has heard the expression often from Lily. And she thinks stern Lily perhaps isn't the liveliest company, a trifle sexless. But Olivia frequently has the same sort of evening herself, sharing a meal with a stranger who has nothing to say and expects a roll in the hay an hour after meeting for the first time. A strong incitement to keep arms and legs crossed. So, Olivia and Lily agree. All they want is to meet a decent man with whom they can have a reasonable sort of life.

Olivia drives home in rush hour to her renovated Victorian in a respectable neighbourhood near the university. The family court judge, astonished at Curtis' multiple sordid addictions, gave her this house, the furniture in it, and custody of the kids. She cooks for them, does the ironing, puts out the garbage. The sun sets in wild violent crimson over the skyline she can see in the distance through her bedroom window. She puts the kids to bed tenderly in the red light, pours another glass of Chardonnay and scrolls through her laptop.

She sends an email to her brother in Calgary. She thinks of her father who died too young when she was a teenager, and her mother who passed away not long after. Then Olivia pays her credit card bill, the gas bill, the cable bill. When they were married, Curtis seldom contributed to the mundane paying of bills, settling this responsibility entirely on her. I bet Kevin makes sure all his family's bills are paid on time. Moving on the screen from her bank's site to Netflix, Olivia looks for something to watch. Nothing appeals. Staring at the screen, she courses through her favourite apps, finds little of interest. She leafs through last month's *Vogue* magazine, briefly skimming an article profiling a British trust fund millionaire, his wife and their villa in Sardinia. She knows her kitchen could use a renovation from top to bottom if she decides to sell and wants to get a good price for the house.

Grabbing her cellphone, she calls Dion, her other best girlfriend from the office. Everything's jumbo-sized about Dion, bosoms, legs, derrière. They try out new restaurants and go to the movies together. She's a little more unbuttoned than Lily; she and Olivia can joke about things like anal sex. Dion is out with a guy she's been seeing for the last little while, having a wonderful evening.

Do you ever feel like an alien? asks Olivia.

I just wish I was home watchin' TV with him, Dion says. She's fed up with dating, wants a commitment from the guy. None is forthcoming. Olivia worries about Dion. She seems like a strong black woman on the surface, but Olivia suspects an inner softness, a sentimental tolerance for bad male behaviour. Too often, too indulgent. Olivia resolutely values her friends Lily and Dion. They are her bulwark against an increasingly cruel, rapacious world, more voracious and unfriendly with every passing season. Dog-tired, Olivia stares out of her window at the sleeping street. Nothing is moving. Olivia's eyes well with tears; briefly, she cries.

Then she eagerly seeks out sleep, craving sweet oblivion. She understands herself to be utterly and finally alone, as if she had been abandoned on an ice flow.

The guy appears at Olivia's door. He's invited her out for dinner. But they're into it even before she gets her coat on and end up in the bedroom. The dude's six feet of hard muscle. Got to spend his whole life in the gym, she thinks. He heaves and groans on top of her for three dreary minutes. Idly curious afterward, Olivia asks where they're eating. His face goes blank for a second before he speaks. Something important's come up with his work, he tells her. Have to give you a raincheck. Did you get a call? she asks. No, I just forgot, he says. The sensation of distaste is as solid and foul as spoiled meat in her throat. Another heartless excuse for a human being. Olivia cherishes her sense of self-respect. She gets up out of bed, nausea mounting, hands him his trousers, and throws him out of the house, never returns any of his calls or texts.

Next day is Friday at the office. Some of the workers in film distribution go down the street to the bogus Irish pub with its emerald shamrocks and fictitious leprechauns. Kevin has some news. His wife has left him for her boss, a dynamic, hustling ad guy. They've been carrying on for months, she's confessed, going for it in the conference room, on top of the mahogany table they've just used to close a juicy deal.

What are you going to do? Olivia asks.

I don't know.

Well, you can't stay there, Kev.

Would you help me find a place?

Kevin, you're an adult. Find a place yourself.

You're right, of course.

What did you do? Olivia presses.

What do you mean?

You must have done something to make her act like that.

I know, I'm boring.

Olivia notices for the first time that Kevin's eyes are a violet so pale they are almost colorless. He regards her steadily without blinking, with monumental patience.

You can't run yourself down like that, she says.

Kevin agrees.

But you can talk to me anytime you like. I'm your friend.

Kevin thanks her. She *is* a friend. He looks at his watch.

Kevin has to go pick up his kids from school. Olivia is a little surprised how agreeable Kevin is, even in such trying circumstances. Maybe she's been a little hard on him. She wouldn't be committing herself to anything by helping a friend find a new place. Even if he is just an office friend. Besides, he was being so brave about the breakup. Olivia was a wreck for months after her breakup, maybe a year. She's feeling a little guilty about how harsh she was with Kevin so when he asks her to have a look at an apartment he's thinking of renting. She agrees to go along even though it's a long drive out to the burbs.

The place is on the 24th floor of a dingy building overlooking the freeway. It stands brutally empty, looks even worse with winter's coming now and snow starting to fall. Not very promising.

This is awful, says Olivia, thinking *another pauperish guy*.

Kevin stands there in his self-consciously reticent grey suit. It's all I can afford right now. I can't let Rebecca down with the household expenses.

Olivia for the first time notices Kevin's stubborn jaw. *But Rebecca betrayed you*, she wants to say. She thinks of lending Kevin some money, then rejects the idea. But she rebukes herself. She's becoming so mistrustful and suspicious lately, always on guard. There's a lonely mirror still hanging on the living room wall. Olivia carefully adjusts her tight-fitting beige sweater.

Kevin says, I want my kids to have the best.

Well, says Olivia, I suppose this will have to do.

Then he startles her by taking her hand.

What are you doing? she asks.

I'm in love with you, Olivia.

Don't be ridiculous, she replies, baffled and outraged by his sudden declaration.

Kevin leaves to take his kids to their little league game. Olivia suddenly feels very tired.

Later Olivia tells Dion on the phone that she thinks Kevin expected her to make love to him right there on the floor in the empty apartment. Dion and Lily are her only confidantes. When Curtis had the hot pants fling that killed off their marriage for good, all of their other friends, in on the secret themselves, had been content to let her flounder in foolish ignorance. She subsequently found it difficult to hold a conversation with them once the truth emerged.

Mmm, kinky, says Dion about the empty apartment and the amorous Kevin.

He doesn't even have a bed. He must think I'm desperate.

Well, aren't you?

Not *that* desperate, says Olivia. But she envisions the scene in the vacant apartment, up against the wall, Kevin's trousers around his ankles, her bare leg hooked around his back.

Hot, maybe?

So, over the next few weeks, Olivia goes to lunch with Kevin frequently, picking up the cheque each time. Christmas is coming, and the boys and girls from the office canyons nearby flood into the neon-lit bar in their down coats and parkas, laughing, ready for single-malt whiskeys and exotic martinis. Olivia sticks to Chardonnay, and Kevin drinks his beer. He pours out his heart about the separation, his kids, his all-encompassing pain at his wife's treachery. It's a time for families, and what a mess his has become. Poor Kevin is as plain and ordinary as yesterday's leftover meatloaf, she thinks, but you can rely on him. Maybe rockin', rollin', tattooed Curtis was okay for the girl she had been. The years had conspired to forever destroy that girl, the willing conspirator of a wild boy. Now, maybe too late, she is ready to settle down to an adult life. Finally, she packs Nicholas and Emily off on a sleepover and invites Kevin to dinner.

She's put up a Christmas wreath on her front door and hung mistletoe over the entrance to the kitchen. When he arrives with two bottles of red wine, Kevin insists on cooking dinner, just to give her a break. It's one of those basic dishes that men who can cook pride themselves on – spaghetti Bolognese – but Olivia appreciates the gesture as well as the small but thoughtful gift of earrings he gives her. Kevin's replaced his perennial suit with checkered pants and a sweater that looks like its been knitted by his aunt in Kitchener, but the tie remains firmly in place. They talk of the office, about miserly Denton Frame's latest round of personnel cuts and how lucky they both were to dodge the bullet. They speak compulsively about Denton, their boss, a former Marxist professor with his white ponytail and red face. Their livelihoods depend on his whims. Each of them could be on the street within days if they crossed one of his many red lines. They talk of his short fuse, his lawsuits, and what a miracle it is that Frames stays afloat on the distribution of Norwegian cable series, Czech dramas, documentaries on the Inuit, tardy payment of bills due and the like. Kevin complains about what a straight arrow the guy is, how he's shown him several creative ways the company could pay less tax, but Denton insists on "giving back," paying his fair socialist share toward the general welfare.

After the meal is finished, they clean up the dishes together. Then Kevin stretches out, shoes off, on her sofa. Olivia allows him to smoke a single cigarette. They've polished off the first bottle of wine and make a solid dent in the second. Olivia sits beside Kevin on the couch, puts a hand on his checkered knee and purposively fiddles with the knot of his blue and red striped tie.

So Kevin, she asks, what does your lawyer say?

About what?

Your divorce, what else?

I haven't talked to a lawyer yet.

Olivia is taken aback. The situation is drifting; in her personal life as in her professional business career, she stubbornly insists matters *move forward*. Olivia has another rule: no affairs with married men.

What are we doing here, anyhow?

I don't get what you mean.

Of course you don't.

Olivia is beginning to feel the wine, perceives herself teetering on the edge of a precipice. All at once, she remembers her early wild days with Curtis, the untrammelled freedom, no rules or boundaries. Once, flush with money from a record session, he had taken her without a moment's notice for a week in Paris. She feels an abject sense of loss. What is she doing with a pedestrian type like Kevin? Then, green eyes blazing, ignoring the vertigo, Olivia proceeds to jump into space.

Marriage, divorce, lawyers, she tells him, who cares? How bourgeois! Why don't we just drive to the airport, go somewhere with a beach, and just enjoy the hell out of each other?

Kevin says he can't just take off, that his boy has hockey practice early tomorrow morning. Olivia just loses it, and as with the muscle man, throws him out of her house. It's getting to be a habit, she thinks, staring at the mistletoe, ten minutes after his car rumbles out of her driveway. The second time in six months. She recalls how Curtis after the divorce dove deep into the twelve steps, AA all the way. Now he lives clean and sobre on a rocky coast in Nova Scotia with a nurse he met in rehab.

Olivia remembers Curtis singing,

I ain't goin' down
That big road,

By myself.

For a moment she looks out the window at her lilacs bordering the sidewalk, bare with winter. She picks up her cellphone and calls Kevin in his car. She persuades him to come back to the house. Leading him to the bedroom, Olivia unbuttons his shirt and moves to his belt. To her shock, Kevin makes love with an eager, furious, insatiable passion. She never would have believed such vehement demons lurked inside that bland persona. Such strength and lurid invention. Holy shit.

In the early dawn, completely spent, he summons the last bit of stamina necessary to take the boy to the rink.

A sated Olivia sleeps for a couple of hours, before waking Lily.

Kevin made love to me five times last night, she says.

My God, says Lily. He didn't. The first time you had sex?

Why not the first time, Olivia thinks.

Is that one of *your* rules, she says. Not too much screwing the first time?

Sometimes Olivia thinks there's such a thing as too many rules.

Lily proceeds to extract every last intimate detail from Olivia's wild night. Olivia detects a note of spinsterly disapproval from her friend. But Olivia, despite herself, is only too happy to confide, secretly proud and even boastful, of having achieved such a sensual feat. She phones Dion too but can't get hold of her. When she does, her friend seems brusque, uninterested.

The holiday season comes and goes. Olivia, packing the kids off on sleepovers, continues to entertain Kevin in the evenings. After a succession of mad midnights, she's beginning to forget his lacks. Somehow they never make it to his lonely bachelor pad; in addition, she's made up her mind never again to enquire after the state of his divorce. But the affair continues, even though he never spends the night, because he's so committed to taking his kids to school in the mornings. She begins to regard him with indulgent affection. A couple weeks later, Lily approaches her at work with shocking news. Checking her online dating apps, she had seen one with a blurred photo of a guy who seemed appealing. Loved kids, pets, home renovation, not fooling around, serious about finding an enduring relationship with a like-minded woman. Lily had made arrangements to meet and guess who turns up? Kevin H. Book! When he saw that his new date was Olivia's best friend, he beat a hasty retreat, she says. She certainly gave him a piece of her mind. He was blushing like crazy.

Olivia tells Lily they had no committed relationship. Kevin was free to do as he liked. So was she.

Don't be so easy on the bastard, says Lily. He's messing you around big time. I was furious for you!

Olivia can see Kevin at a workstation in their hot desk office. She decides to say nothing just at the moment but starts to do a little digital computer work. She moves to her screen. As head of IT, she has access to the computer of every Frames employee. It's not exactly inside the guidelines of the company's code of personal ethics, but she hacks her way into Kevin's email. Olivia is astonished by what she finds there. Not just his emails to herself and Lily but also emails to several other women – including Dion who's he's apparently been seeing for months. And Rebecca. And his wife, with whom he's apparently on very good terms.

Kevin to Dion: One to remember. See you after I drop the kid off.

To Rebecca: What an anniversary! How could a guy be so lucky?

To Olivia herself: I bless the day I met you. Got to go to Home Hardware. But, later?

Olivia feels once again like an alien life form arriving on a new planet. Secrecy is difficult in a hot desk office where so many work tables are shared. She sends emails to Lily and Dion. She invites

Dion to lunch at the trattoria a couple of blocks away. Over a bowl of pasta, Olivia makes certain that Dion has read Kevin's emails. She mockingly reads aloud from her cellphone a few of the choice email exchanges. Olivia's friend is sullen, unbelieving, unyielding. She seems angrier with her than with Kevin. She toys with the rings on her hands, then draws herself up regally, which is something Olivia's never seen before.

Why didn't you tell me about him? asks Olivia.

Weren't none of your business.

It makes me crazy.

Dion shrugs.

Treats me fine. You're just jealous. Dion gets up from the table, turns her back on Olivia and heads for the ladies', where she stays. Olivia realizes that it was Kevin Dion was telling her about on the phone that night. Kevin was the guy she wanted to be cozying up with watching TV, instead of out on the town.

Back at the office on her laptop, Olivia plunders Kevin's HR file for his old address. It's not a house in Mississauga but a luxury condo overlooking the lake. She's decided to have a word with Kevin's wife Rebecca.

That evening she arrives at the front door on the 45th floor. The elevator opens directly into the penthouse apartment. Rebecca is very tall, ten years older than Kevin. Hair tinted a dark red, hazel eyes. A teenage boy's chest. She smokes a cigarette in an ebony holder and wears a louche black silk robe. Two Irish setters cavort around her legs. Olivia feels a quick knife thrust of envy: Kevin's wife's condo is like something out of one of her *Vogue* magazines. There's a painting by a Mexican muralist that Olivia has been seeing in prints all her life; the painting should be in a museum, but here it is on Rebecca's living room wall. The penthouse – filled with large Italian urns, framed posters from national ad campaigns, chinoiserie up the wazoo – sports a panoramic view of the lake.

Rebecca politely invites her in. She listens, unsmiling and eye-brow arched, to Olivia's prosecutor's brief. The cocktail in her elegant hand is clearly not the first or even the third of the evening. Beyond her, a flat screen blares out a cable series from BBC on Netflix. Rebecca looks Olivia up and down as if itemizing her demeanour and and pricing every item of her clothing. Apparently, she is not impressed, and her lip curls savagely downward. She's neglected to offer Olivia even so much as a glass of water, much less what she's been drinking all evening.

You're one of those pathetic women from his work? she asks, stumbling slightly. No, hang on a moment, I know who you are. You're another rare spirit left yearning and forsaken.

There are guttural traces of a European accent. She seems inordinately pleased with her bon mot.

He said you were getting divorced.

As far as I know, Rebecca slurs, Kevin still lives here. We're married.

How can that be?

My dear, Kevin may come home late, but he always comes home.

Looking beyond Rebecca's shoulder, Olivia peers into the condo. There is no evidence of family life. No toys, bicycles, schoolbooks, hockey sweaters. Nada. No sign of children whatsoever.

What about the kids?

What kids?

The ones he's always taking to the rink!

I can't have children, glares Rebecca, the black silk robe slipping loose. I don't care for them anyhow.

It's as if her barrenness were Olivia's fault. She wonders what perversity, what theory of marriage leads Rebecca to live in these circumstances. And what appetites drive Kevin to navigate such a web of lies. And how to ask a complete stranger such questions?

Rebecca shows Olivia the door. Perhaps this isn't the first time one of Kevin's dupes has come calling. What kind of humans have I landed amongst, Olivia asks herself. Driving home, she wonders how trust gradually seeped out of her life only to be replaced by suspicion. Every day hustlers tried their moves by phone and email, looking for marks. Kevin with his sly manoeuvers, and now her office friends, his prey. She saw why the people around her retreated into their families as if behind fortress walls. But what was she, with no family except Nicholas and Emily, supposed to do? It was like she had been left on the battlefield with no cover. She didn't want to become hardened and armoured, but to do otherwise left her vulnerable to marauders like Kevin H. Book.

She summons Lily and Dion to a late-night confab at her house. She finds it hard to believe that three bright women have bought such a stale pitch from Kevin: *my marriage is in trouble, my wife is awful, please help.* What a salesman! After a couple bottles of Chardonnay and two hours of loud argument, Olivia convinces them to confront Kevin. So, Dion makes a dinner date at a chic restaurant in the entertainment district, promising a big night on her. The three of them arrive early and are shown to their table. They order drinks. Kevin arrives ten minutes late, in his best suit, looking like a barber dressed up for Sunday. He arrives at the table with a big white smile. When he sees the three reproachful faces, his eyes widen and the smile disappears.

I'm sorry, he says.

Is that all you have to say? asks Olivia.

Wait until we inform Denton what you've done, says Lily, a blush of rage showing on her olive cheek. You'll be on the street. Bet your life on that, mister. We'll make you our special project, our hobby.

Dion says more directly, I oughta kick your ass.

Kevin actually sneers like a cartoon villain. This is the first time Olivia has seen him with such an expression. Like he's an entirely different person.

Kevin says, I don't have to take this.

He turns on his heel and leaves the restaurant. The three women regard each other blankly.

He couldn't get out of here fast enough, says Olivia.

Just what I expected, says Dion.

He did apologize, says Lily.

Don't make excuses for the little bastard, says Olivia. Did you see his expression?

Horrific, says Lily.

Like an animal, says Dion.

A snake, says Olivia.

The conversation pauses as they all reflect on what just happened.

Let's have dinner anyhow, says Lily, straining to be cheerful. Dion is already perusing the menu enthusiastically.

Suddenly, I'm not so hungry, Olivia says. She heads out into the relentless neon glare and walks away from the restaurant.

This can't go on, this can't go on, one day soon I'll meet somebody – not some cheap salesman like Kevin or a wandering player like Curtis – and he'll be strong and he'll do what he says he will do and we'll travel the world, and even if he has kids he'll treat Nicholas and Emily as if they were his own, and he'll be open with me, and he'll be a free spirit too, and I'll teach him to enjoy the finer things, and our love will last forever. And when I meet this new man, I will force him to understand me as a woman of carnal secrets, passion and resourcefulness.

With spring still weeks away, cold winds whistle through the towers of glass and steel as Olivia hurries down into the subway that will take her home to her kids. After paying the fare, she waits on the well-lit platform with the rest of the crowd. When the train arrives and the doors slide open, she steps through into the silver car.

Olivia rests her head against the window. She remembers the trip she and Curtis took to Mexico when they first met. The heat, the dusty brown hills, the bougainvillea, the flower markets. They were happy and in love. Irrefutably, she has known ecstatic triumph. Secure in this womanly certainty, she knows she will triumph again.

Linda Rogers

BREAKING THE SOUND BARRIER

I always look under the bed. Never know when I might find a pastry pincher hiding with a fresh pie, a pair of ruby spirit guides (no place like home), or the stranger who will force me because nice girls say no even when they mean yes.

Our room for this night of all nights, first sleep of the first year in the age of American unexceptionalism, belongs to our host. I get down on my knees and inhale the toxic flakes of skin that lurk in shared bedrooms, then sneeze, blow some to the other side of the bed, vibrating a handful of strings in the key of C.

This time the black home of dust bunnies is filled with an angel harp, tuned, I imagine, ready, a big one for a big seraph, one of the choir who plays high notes at night, *da capo*, so that when I wake up tomorrow, I will be dead.

I fold the stiff sheets back and tiptoe in. Things take longer to start in the winter: the car, birdsong, lust. I don't want to disturb our invisible messenger until he's ready to sing.

When you take the plunge a few minutes later, your cold hand explores my fretless spine. Did you wonder what I might wear for the New Year? This is your answer. Nothing. The deep-freeze. Nothing but goosebumps.

No carolling from me, as you might have expected. I am not dressed in sequins and feathers, ready for an organ recital.

I can't see you pout in the dark, but no doubt you are pouting. You like the mystery of layers, layers of silk, mysterious barricades (your favourite piece of music) to overcome. I get it. I've had my fist up sheep vaginas, sorted out their young, feet, noses, bottoms, in the softest and warmest of tissues.

─↗↖─

We drove through a storm this afternoon over the Malahat, where snowflakes as big as our hands thumped the windshield. Flying blind, we try to hear the news on the radio.

"This is crap," you said, because you are an apostate cantor. No heaven here, no glorious hereafter. Just the Asperger weather channel, the worst scenario.

I used to believe in God, the weather his method of excretion, executive execution. Far away in the Caribbean, an airplane might be unloading its toilet on a cruise ship. What would the tourists be thinking?

No airplanes or angels flew over the Malahat this afternoon, but we did get out of the car, undress and lie down in the snow.

─↗↖─

Later at midnight, while naked women all over the world lay on their backs making wings, a banjo angel came into the club and sat down beside you to play the blues.

I shivered in the dark while his breath extinguished the faltering candles and you segued into the break, mandolin versus banjo.

You are too easily seduced by these sky riders, all your chakras rising. Bass takeoff, mezzo cloud formations, and treble flight. But you always come back.

Snow returns to dark reservoirs, white ravens downsize to crows. I watch you melt into the music, into black holes between the notes. That's why I won't say Love. Love melts. It is the temperature of transformation, when stars become sand and eventually glass shatters beneath the bridegroom's foot or under the weight of snow.

—)\(—

"That was dangerous," I say, meaning your improvised ghost duet. I was breathing for both of us in case you forgot while your fingers danced over those twinned arpeggios, your *pas de deux*.

"Lots of soul," I say, because I am generous, because as soon as you wrap your whole self around me, I will be warm. "Stinct" as the dead poet liked to say, as opposed to extinct.

"I thought he was dead," I say.

"So did he, apparently. He told me about his near-death experience."

"I know about that. I've been there, the cloud tunnel." It's an old story a criminally sloppy doctor, the dead chorister I followed to the very steps of heaven, my child.

"Well, it was different for him. While he was floating into the wild blue yonder, there were angels with banjos sitting on every cloud. He said they told him to take dictation."

"I thought the banjo players all went to hell."

"Apparently not," he said. It was definitely heaven, and there were lots of banjos: tenor banjos, five string banjos, banjo mandolins, fretless banjos, you name it. He had to memorize all the parts because he didn't have pencil and paper.

"Did he try to talk you into going there?" I don't dare venture the other side of the question, *Did you want to go?*

"I'm here aren't I?"

"So, why is he in our room?"

"He isn't."

"Yes, he is. His harp is under the bed."

"You must be kidding. Besides, you were there, he played banjo."

"See for yourself."

"You want me to look because there might be a harp lurking there?"

"That's right. Nothing unusual. How many mandolins have you stashed under our bed?"

"That's different. This is a hotel."

"NO it isn't. It's a B & B."

"What's the difference?"

"A hotel is a tower of bunks and a B & B is a drink made by monks."

You roll onto me, cover my breasts with both hands and, we spoon. I have read that cuddles are therapeutic, the best cure for anxiety and loneliness. It's true, and I know we are both released, you to music and me to words, the usual. Neither of us makes a sound, apart from our breathing.

꘎

"Stop!" A voice in the dark startles us from semi-consciousness. We open our eyes and turn to the beautiful light outlining the shape of a person.

"It's him," I say.

"Who?

"The dead banjo player."

"This is crazy."

"Tell him to fuck off," I say. "He had his chance."

If it weren't so damned cold, I would jump out of bed, grab my lipstick and write TAKEN on your naked backside. Music is sex and sex is the portal. One day, you won't come back.

"No, stop. I'm serious," the visitor insists.

"The score's love all," I mutter, sliding into a still-cold part of the bed, my martyr position. I will be cold and alone, the death rehearsal. You will be sorry. "Asshole."

You say nothing. Okay, you are shocked, maybe suspending disbelief.

"You could tell him to leave."

"I didn't ask him here, and I locked the door when I came to bed."

"Are you saying what I think you're saying? Is this our Tinker Bell moment?" Now I am fully awake.

"I'm saying I don't know how he got in and I didn't let him in. That's all." My apostate Jew doesn't usually give credence to miracles or mechanical apparitions.

"He's right," the dead man says, or is it the landlord who has forgotten he gave us his bed and stumbled upon us?

"Are you our innkeeper or the invisible musician?"

"The latter."

"So you are dead?" I ask.

"Yes and no. I auditioned but they sent me back. Does that not make sense to you?"

"I guess so. I've been there," I say. "And yes, I was returned to sender."

"That would be your husband."

"Yes."

"He needs you more."

I think of the almost desperate way you play, as if every note were a prayer that counted, what some people call soul. I like to think you need me, which your world depends on, whatever I bring to it: coherence, loyalty, a few laughs.

"Yes. And I need him." That is a warning, husband hijacker in the dark, angel or whatever. I do not look lightly on man filching. "So you can go."

"I'm here to give you a warning."

"What is that?" you ask, your pitch slightly hysterical, a verboten word in our household.

"You are in danger. Don't rock the bed," our visitor orders.

"Malapropism," I say. "It's don't rock the boat. Beds don't rock, they might vibrate under certain circumstances, but they do not rock."

"Don't vibrate the bed."

I ask our guest, "Are you here to initiate a threesome?"

"With humans," you add because you have retrieved your sense of the ridiculous from the sinkhole swallowing us. " If you're a Valkyrie, we're not ready. We still have America to disarm."

"But first we sleep, and you are leaving." I'm getting into the rhythm of this.

"I have to warn you. "

"No, we've been warned. Just go. Please." You are more polite than I. If I thought I could murder an idea or a psalm, this is the time I would try.

He leaves, I think, but not by the window or door. They remain shut.

Minus his aura, the dark goes darker. Blessed relief.

We touch one another to affirm we are still here, count sheep out loud, drift apart, but I hear music on my way out, the little Bach song, "Sheep may safely graze and pasture…"

-~|~-

You usually wake up and tell me your dreams. I am not jealous. Well, maybe I am. Of course I wonder what that is like, making music, making love all day and all night long? I admire your night adventures because they have grand comic twists. That is the gift of men on the Asperger scale, one of the gifts: discomfort, the portal to laughter.

"Would you like me to throw something on and go down-stairs for coffee?"

"Send our guest," you say. "Tell him I want double cream."

"Ha ha. Very funny. Besides, he's gone."

"Oh good."

"I heard a Bach cantata when I was falling asleep."

"Meaning?"

"Did you get up and play that harp in the middle of the night?"

"Now you're being ridiculous."

"Okay, so look under the bed. You promised. Assume the position." I can't wait. You look so pathetic on your hands and knees with your balls dangling between your thighs.

"No problem," you roll out of the sack and kneel beside the bed.

"So look."

You lift the skirt under the mattress, very deliberately, very dramatically. You look. Then, still on all fours, you slowly back up. You whisper, "I want you to get out of bed very carefully, not over the end. Get out on my side, carefully, and slowly walk to the door. Then get out of the way, quick. It isn't a harp."

"Bare naked?" I smirk. Nice try, dude. This is revenge, the teabag twist. I remember the Italians swear on their testicles.

"Doesn't matter. Keep quiet. Move slowly and then get out of the way. Duck and cover."

"Couldn't we go out the window?"

"On the third floor?"

"Okay, okay," I humour him. I slowly get up, tiptoe to the door and open it slowly, carefully. There's no one in the hall, thank God.

"Go!"

"Are we making this up?"

"Probably," he follows me out.

"There was no angel."

"What?"

"That was no harp. There's a loaded crossbow under the bed."

"Cupid?" I slam the door, laugh, and the harp thing goes off with a snappy pow! sound like a bass string snapping, then a gut-twisting thump.

"Sweet Jesus!"

We crawl to the stairs and sit down.

"Are we 'stinct'?" I am tempted to laugh because that has become an ambiguous question.

"I think so."

"What the hell?"

"Could be, with three hundred million armed Americans."

"But this is Canada."

"This is whatever we want it to be."

"You mean that."

"I do." We have a long history of me never backing down.

"I'd rather figure this out with my clothes on. I'm going back in," you say, standing up.

"Me too. Stronger together."

"I love you," we say in unison, after the kiss, turning toward the door. What's to lose? Only our lives. And it will be worth it because we've been given another gig-from-hell story to tell.

Carly Vandergriendt

RESURFACING

The volunteers wait in a cluster on the beach. Thirty or so of them in all. Faces Jackie recognizes, people who've been coming to the Point for a long time. If her mother were here, she'd be nudging her and whispering, *That twit brings his wife up one weekend and his mistress the next.* Or, *Boy did the DeWitt girl ever straighten out.*

The afternoon sun spills across the surface of the lake. You wouldn't know a man drowned here this morning. An out-of-towner. It's always the out-of-towners, thinks Jackie. They don't know about the rip current. It pulls you halfway to Erie, Pennsylvania before you even realize.

"His poor family. How terrible," says Anna. A ladybug lands on her bare shoulder. She flicks it away.

What does Anna know about terrible things? Jackie wonders, glaring. There's a dull ache in her forehead, tucked behind her skull. She was trying to sleep it off when the helicopter started up. It circled for hours. She knew what it meant. After lunch, she told Chris to take their boys to town for the afternoon. Her brother, Jeff, went with them. Anna stayed.

Someone from Norfolk County Fire & Rescue had been by the cottage. A kayaker had gone missing that morning, he told Jackie. They needed help with the search.

The same County volunteer now reappears before the crowd, holding a loudspeaker. "We're going to make a chain," he calls, corralling them.

The group thins out. Anna seizes Jackie's right hand before she can move away. The lady who ends up on her left has a cottage on the channel side. Jackie thinks she was at her mother's funeral.

The County volunteer wades out to a Sea-Doo and revs the engine. He holds the loudspeaker in front of his face, calling them foreward.

It's a slow march into the water. Jackie's arms break out in a rash of goosebumps. The lake is always colder after a storm. And opaque. Brown. Unsettled.

"I kind of hope we don't find him," whispers Anna. "Is that bad?"

"Don't think about it," says Jackie. Though she's thought about it herself. What it might feel like. The waterlogged body. She imagines a certain leadenness, pickled skin. She shivers.

They reach the first sandbar and stagger to a collective stop. Jackie is stretched between Anna and the woman from across the channel. Gentle waves slosh at her knees.

"We're stopping?" Anna pokes her head out and looks down the line.

The last time the Van Leeuwens came to the Point as a family, Jackie was fifteen. Later that year, her dad disappeared. He was gone nine months before he reappeared like it was nothing. He wouldn't say where he'd been. Jackie's mother never got over it.

It probably killed her. But that came later.

Another call from the loudspeaker, and they advance in slow motion. A line of lumbering astronauts. The water is up to Jackie's hips. This is where it drops off, she thinks.

∽

"That's six to four," said Jackie. Smug, because she and Anna were winning. She pushed the cards towards Chris. "Your deal."

Chris didn't care for euchre. Not like the Van Leeuwens. They were a euchre-playing family. That is, when they were still a family. Their mother had been dead now for over a year. Neither Jackie nor Jeff spoke to their father. In fact, they only saw each other once a year when Jackie and Chris brought the kids down from the Ottawa Valley.

"Time out," said Jeff. "Anyone want anything?"

"Another beer," said Chris.

"I'll take a top-up," Jackie said, handing Jeff her glass.

"Nothing for me," said Anna. She rose from the table and walked to the row of windows at the back, looking out at the shifting darkness that was the lake.

"You sure?" called Jackie. All of the windows were shut, but the sound of roaring the wind and crashing waves filled the cottage.

Anna didn't answer.

Jackie tried to exchange an eye-roll with Chris, but he was caught up dealing the next hand. On his face, the same look of forced concentration Cole made when he read. She smiled at the thought of their eldest son. Buoyed by two glasses of white wine and several rum and cokes, she could forget the fight he'd put up about brushing his teeth. And Felix, her sweet baby. Maybe he wouldn't cry for her later on that night. Alcohol made raising kids seem only mildly awful.

Chris doled out four neat piles of five cards. He put the kitty in the middle of the table and turned over the top card.

"Not yet," whispered Jackie. "Jeff'll murder you."

He turned the card back over. Under the table, she rubbed a clumsy foot against his. God, she loved him. For stepping in when Cole got mouthy. For playing euchre. For making an effort with Jeff and his fun-sponge of a girlfriend. Anna wouldn't even have a drink, now what was that about? She was too thin to be pregnant. When Jeff brought her last year, Jackie hadn't paid much attention because Jeff's relationships never lasted. He didn't even have a type. Women, plural. That used to be his type.

Jackie studied Anna as she returned to the table. Tall and gawky, with that thing all the twentysomething women were talking about. A thigh gap. Jackie's thighs were dimpled and doughy, like *oliebollen* batter. They probably hadn't *not* touched since 1988.

"Windy out there," said Anna.

"Gearing up for a storm," said Jeff. He smiled, set the drinks on the table, and took his seat next to Jackie. Jeff wasn't some megastud, thought Jackie. He was just a likeable guy. He should have been bored with Anna by now.

"Erie likes to show off," Jackie added. A distant clap of thunder sounded, as if to prove her point.

"I guess that's our cue," said Chris. "Game on."

"Yes sir," said Jeff.

Chris turned over the upcard. They lifted their cards to their chests. For a second, Jackie imagined Jim-and-Janet and Jeff-and-Jackie circa 1982. Bound to each other by some invisible force, they sat in the shadowy living room of the cottage, playing out yet another summer storm.

Jackie had a dismal hand. Three nines, two queens, and only one of every single suit. She passed. The others did too. Jeff and Chris took five tricks that hand, tying the game six-six. It was Jackie's turn to deal.

"Do you remember," started Jeff, "when Mom used to go away for the weekend and we'd stage those euchre tournaments in the basement?"

Now, whenever they were together, they ended up reminiscing about that parentless time. Adulthood had set Jeff and Jackie had drifted apart. That parentless time was all they had.

"Marty lost his old junker in a bet," said Jackie, as she dealt the cards, "and on Monday morning his dad showed up at school to beg Jerry De Vries to give it back."

"Where was your mom?" asked Anna.

Jackie bristled as she turned over the queen of spades.

"Our Dad left," Jeff explained. Not *missing* or *lost*. Just left. As if the real leaving came then and not later. "When he left, she would go around to different cities showing his picture to people."

"She just left you two alone?" asked Anna. White lightning filled the cottage, illuminating the freckles on her nose.

"It was the 80s," said Jeff. "Things were different then."

"To be fair," Jackie cut in, "Jeff was seventeen. He should have been capable of looking after me. Instead he started an illegal gambling operation in our basement."

"Well, what about that babysitter Mom hired?" asked Jeff. "She wasn't exactly going out of her way to stop me. Pass, by the way."

Jeff always brought up the babysitter, Jackie thought. Did he know? She studied her hand. She had both bowers. If she picked up that queen, she could go this round alone. That'd be four points and a win for her team. That'd show Jeff.

"She was nineteen," said Jackie.

"Pass," said Anna.

"Pass," said Chris, his eyes on his cards. "What was her name again?"

"Sharon," said Jackie, off-handedly. "Spades." She picked up the queen. "I'm going to go it alone."

Anna sighed as she set her cards face-down on the table.

"Winner gets the loser's car," said Jeff, playing the ace of diamonds. Chris followed suit with a jack.

"You want our minivan?" asked Jackie, taking the trick. "You can have it."

"You know she was at Mom's funeral."

"Who?"

"Sharon."

"I know," snapped Jackie. Seeing Sharon at the funeral had sparked a small-scale, pre-midlife crisis during which Jackie began compulsively noticing women. There was Cole's teacher, a sinewy woman with a mop of tight brown curls. There was the blonde woman from the Office of External Relations with the New-Agey name Jackie could never remember. What did Jackie like? She had no clue. Once, she had liked Sharon.

"She looked," said Jeff. "different. Don't you think?"

"I'd hope. Twenty years later," said Jackie. What was he getting at? "Look. Can we, like, drop the babysitter thing?"

"I thought you guys were friends?"

"Why would I be friends with our old babysitter?"

She slapped the left bower down. Jeff laid a low spade, Chris an ace. Jackie took the trick. Three more tricks, and she'd get her four points. She looked at Anna, who was sitting with her chin propped on her hands, a yawn about to slide across her face.

"You were so close back then."

"Still friends with everyone from back then?" Wrong question, Jackie knew immediately. Jeff had never left their hometown.

"Don't get so worked up."

Her brother was the only person in the world who could use that line. And it worked. Now, she couldn't deny being worked up without sounding worked up. Jackie had a thought, then. A boozy thought. What if she told him?

She played the right bower. "You know what," she started.

"What?" asked Jeff, laying down an off-suit card.

Chris hesitantly showed diamond. Jackie took her third trick.

"Sharon and I—" continued Jackie. She had to play a card first. King of spades or king of clubs? She chose the spade.

"Yes?"

"We were girlfriends." No, thought Jackie. That wasn't right. Not girlfriends – she has girlfriends now. Female friends, that is. "We were. Together."

"What?"

"We were," she hesitated "romantic."

Jeff scrunched his brow. He set the jack of diamonds down. Chris played a nine, and Jackie took a fourth trick. She lifted her chin as she swept up the cards, noticing Anna was staring at her.

"You were, what, fifteen? Isn't that kind of wrong?" Jeff paused. "She took advantage of you."

"Right," said Jackie. At the funeral, the four years between them seemed utterly insignificant. "Because you never dated anyone that young when you were nineteen."

Another clap of thunder sent the plates clinking in the cupboards. Felix would be awake soon, thought Jackie. She played her last card.

"That's different," said Jeff. "I mean, at that age. How could you know?" He played a low diamond, and looked to Chris. "Did you know about this?"

"What does it have to do with him?" asked Jackie. She heard a moan from the boys' room.

"Yeah," Chris answered, clutching his last card. "I knew."

"And it doesn't bother you?"

"Why would it?" asked Chris. He set the card down. The ace of clubs. So Chris had the ace. He took the trick, as Felix erupted into a full-fledged wail.

"Then I guess everything worked out," said Jeff, looking from Jackie to Chris and back. He swiped the cards into a messy pile. "What is that now? Seven to six?"

Jackie frowned. "What's that supposed to mean?"

"It means you didn't get your four points," said Jeff.

"No," said Jackie. "You guess everything worked out? You mean I didn't end up with Sharon? You mean I'm not—" Jackie stopped herself. She stood up and left the table.

The darkness in the boys' room was disorienting. "Mummy's here," she whispered. She padded her way to the bottom bunk and fit her body next to Felix's, lifting his pyjama to rub the hot skin on his back. "Shhh," she murmured.

Sharon had left for university around the same time Jackie's father reappeared. For months, Jackie wrote her long-winded letters in blue ink, the ballpoint tip tearing through the paper while her mother's voice spilled from the family room, husky and bitter. *Tell me. Where did you go?* But Jackie never heard a response.

Eventually, Sharon stopped writing back.

After a few minutes, Jackie could feel her son's small body letting go, his awareness receding. His breathing slowed. She wouldn't be like her own mother. She wouldn't abandon her children before they were ready.

Jackie got over Sharon. She moved to Ottawa to go to university, where she met Chris. She married and thought little of the past. Her father's disappearance and his refusal to talk about it, had wedged itself like a stake between the members of the Van Leeuwen family. Her parents divorced, and Jackie had her own kids. When her mother got sick, she found she wanted to tell her about Sharon. She wanted to say, *This is what was happening then, and you had no idea.*

But she didn't.

Jackie hadn't realized she'd dozed off until the door opened. There was someone in the doorway.

"Chris?" she muttered.

From the bed, Jackie saw the hall light silhouetting Anna's thighs, the space between them glowing. She sat up, startled.

∞

They're up to their midriffs now, their linked hands suspended above the surface. Jackie looks back. The pastel-coloured cottages are strung out like beads on a candy necklace.

"I wonder," says Anna. "how much farther we can walk."

"Erie is shallow," says Jackie. "There's a second sand bar." They used to make it as far as kids. Then their mother would stand on the beach and holler into the wind for them to come in. Because that's what mothers are supposed to do, and that's what Jackie's mother had always done. Until her husband left and she just stopped. Hollering. Caring.

"What I don't get," starts Anna, "is how a full-grown man gets pulled under here?"

"That's it," says Jackie. "The current doesn't pull you under. It pulls you out. You get tired. And then—"

"Oh," says Anna.

"It happens every year."

"You mean, people drown?"

"Yeah."

"Jeff never mentioned that."

"Mr. Positive," says Jackie.

"I know."

Jackie waits for her to say more.

"Jeff is great."

"Yeah?"

"It's just… I don't know if he told you? But I'm on an antidepressants. It makes me kind of. Not myself," says Anna.

Is she talking about last night? wonders Jackie.

"It's like. Sometimes I do things and I just don't care about the consequences."

Jackie was still foggy with sleep when Anna sat down on the bed. Her hand grazed Jackie's leg, ever so lightly. Jackie's heat felt like shame, her son sleeping next to her in the bed. She stood up. Dizziness caught her as Anna left the room.

The water laps at her collarbone. Around them, the chain is breaking. The lady from the channel side lapses into a doggie paddle. Jackie pulls her hand from Anna's, lifts her feet from the sandy bottom. That's when she sees it. A flash of something pale between the waves. Driftwood, thinks Jackie, because dead bodies don't float. Or do they?

"Can you see that?"

"What?" asks Anna. Her head is still above the water, her feet still planted.

"There's something there." Treading, Jackie points. The more she studies it, the more it looks like a limb. An arm, maybe.

"I see it," says Anna.

Jackie kicks. Her foot jabs at sand. It's getting shallower. She can stand again.

"Come forward," calls the County volunteer.

They walk until they hit an incline. The second sandbar. The water level drops to their ribs now. Jackie keeps her eyes fixed on the floating thing. If it's actually part of a body, wouldn't the helicopter have spotted it, protruding from the water like that? It catches the sunlight, slick and shining.

"Stop. Let's re-form the chain."

Anna extends her hand. Jackie hesitates, takes it.

"Should we say something?" asks Anna.

Before Jackie can answer, they're moving forward again. It's just a piece of wood, she tells herself. Likely blew in with the storm. So why isn't it drifting closer? It disappears, resurfacing in the same place, about twenty feet away, a moment later.

She finds herself thinking about the man. *His poor family.* Are his loved ones out searching? There are times when she wishes her own father had stayed lost. Her mother would have called off the search. Fifteen feet now. She is almost sure – it isn't. Him. But the way it moves. Fluid-like. Not bobbing. Not like driftwood. Ten feet. Jackie tightens her grip on Anna's hand. The women on either side tug her along until she stops, digging her heels into the sand. The chain bows around her. At last, she sees the illusion. It's just a branch. A piece of driftwood masquerading as a man's arm.

Seán Virgo

SWEETIE

"I know you from somewhere," she said, and stood looking at me as though she expected an answer.

Talking to someone in a mirror is a weird dimension, even in the most familiar moments. Some people do that every day. Hairdressers, makeup artists. I wonder what their dreams are like.

I was drying my hands, and saw myself looking puzzled. "I don't think so," I said. Had she followed me to the washroom? I don't know. Several times I'd glanced up from our meal and found her eyes meeting mine across the room – casual enough but too often, perhaps, for coincidence.

She came closer in the mirror, her heels loud in that bright, confined space. "I don't forget faces," she said. "Was it Banff? Sundance?" She was vivid, I think to be the word. Daring, demanding eyes and, just on the wild side of elegance, her mouth, her hair.

I love the old notion that vampires don't show in a mirror, except that I've always wondered *but what about their clothes?* (And when you think about it, that could be even more spooky.) Her suit was dark navy, and tailored, with a string of black oval beads at her throat. A soft collar flared white over the lapels. Pricey stuff. "No," I told her, "I really don't think we've met." And there we were, almost side by side in the glass, watching each other, at the start or more likely the end of a conversation.

My first lover and I, when I was seventeen, used to stand naked in front of the mirror in his mom's room, and talk to each other. We'd touch sometimes, but mostly we talked and watched because when we touched, the third dimension would break in. And that's the thing – the moment you turn to each other in the actual air, it's like surfacing. Smell, taste, the senses all come back to life. It's so *immediate*.

It was when I stepped back from the wash basins and glanced at her sideways, that something about her cheekbones, the slight bulge of her eyes, made me stop. The full lower lip too. "No, you're right, "I said. "I do remember," and I searched for the name— "Weren't you Annie, Andrea...?"

"Angela," she said to the mirror. "And I still am. Angela Porelli. Soft Touch Productions. So, where was it? You're ahead of me here."

"No, no," I said, the words and the memory coming as one, for that's how it happens, doesn't it – the spoken words running ahead somehow, the thought catching up just in time? "It was in Tideswell, when we were kids – yes, Angela, Angie." I nearly said "Boobsy," that world flooding back at me.

She turned to face me. "Mercy, Lord," she said, and narrowed her eyes. "You were one of Ray Coulter's crew."

Then I saw something like cruelty in her features, though she charmed it away in an instant. There were people out there, I was sure, who knew that look well.

"He was my uncle," I said. "And your dad used to bring us eggs when we visited." I remembered the old van, rattling down the driveway. "And your name was Milton then, right?"

"Milton's was the farm's name, sweetie. Our's was Beaupré." She folded her arms; her cleavage was still a feature. "That's going a long way back," she said, and eyed me up and down. She looked into my face, and then at the mirror, and back again. "Don't tell me you were that tomboy who wouldn't wear skirts."

That was true enough. I laughed. I'd been a girl between two brothers, terrified of losing them to my womanhood. "Stephanie," I said. "It was Stevie of course, back then."

"Well, let me look at you now." She reached out and took hold of my arms. Her hands weren't attractive; the nails had dark polish on them, with two big clunky rings on her wedding finger. There was a bouquet of perfume and wine half as big as the Ritz. "Why, you're gorgeous," she said. "Whoever would have imagined?"

I don't take orders kindly, and condescension even less. And I don't like people who loom at me. I stepped back from her clutches.

"Wait, wait now," she said, lifting hands in a mock surrender. "Do you live in town?"

I told her I was just visiting. And I asked if she still went back home.

"I left that dump when I was seventeen, darling, never to return. I could buy the whole place now if I wanted to, twenty times over."

I had to ask, of course.

"TV production, sweetie. And I'm good at it. *Payback*, remember that? – still running in sixteen countries. And *Bloodlines* season two in the can – with Misha Kapoyan and my precious Antonia. The feuding immigrants." Her energy crowded the washroom.

"I might have caught an episode," I said, "in a hotel room once."

"Oh, spare me," she groaned. "Don't tell me you're one of those pignuts who pride themselves on not having television?"

"It's not pride," I said. "It's boredom."

"Well, la," she said, and turned to the mirror. She fished out a compact and lipstick and leaned over the basin. "Anyway," she said, "you're quite right, it's all fluff. But it pays the bills, my darling, and it gets us known." She worked on her lashes. "And you'll take our next project seriously, believe me. We're pitching it to HBO next month and they'll bite. It's a class act, original, cutting edge. White slavery. The bad guys are the good guys. All the angles."

She was big from behind, though the clothes made the best of that. She hadn't looked after herself, and she knew it of course. That's where the flash and sparkle came in, I suppose. But there was a delicacy in the way she stroked on the lipstick, and then closed her eyes for a moment in the glass. A young woman surfaced, and I was wondering what *her* dreams must be like, when she whirled around, snapping her purse shut, all eyes and pizzazz.

"So," and she flexed her fingers, wriggling them like a pianist over the keyboard, "tell me. Husbands? Kids? The story so far?"

"One died, one left me. The husbands, I mean." It was the kind of thing she might have said. I didn't like myself for it.

"Mine's a gem," she said. "I couldn't do a damn thing without him." She had that off by heart.

"And I've a daughter, seventeen," I said. "And I write for a living – well, living and partly living."

"We always need writers, lovey," she said. "We must talk sometime. And the swellegant beau buying you lunch?"

"No, that's Nicky," I said. "You know, my little brother who you took in hand, remember?" I almost laughed out loud, and felt the balance shift between us, but she just shrugged. Well, maybe she didn't remember, who knows?

"I'd better get back to him anyway," I said, and made for the door.

"I'll come say helloski," she said, and then as I was leaving, "What's that Ray doing these days?"

"Living and partly living," I said. "He got the dotty genes. He's in a home." I can be a bitch, but I hate hearing myself sound like one. I stood for a moment outside the washroom, wishing the last five minutes away. But on my way back to the table, I started to smile. Nick raised an eyebrow.

"What's up?" he asked

"You'll never guess who I just met in the washroom."

"The queen bee," he said. "I saw her go in just after you."

"The queen bee?" (though I could see at once how it might fit her).

"I've been watching them all through the meal," he said, leaning forward. "She's holding court, and they're totally under her thumb, except that other woman might have a mind of her own." That other woman was watching us, as it happened, with a faint smile on her lips. She met my eyes calmly, with a slight nod, and turned back to her companions. The men at the table were like schoolboys in Cadillac suits, full of wine and themselves

"It's Boobsy from Tideswell," I told him. "Remember, Nicky?" and then he looked up, and her hand was on my shoulder.

"Parli del diavolo e compare!" she declaimed, in what seemed like a perfect accent. Everyone at her table was watching, but then so were the diners at the other tables. "*Liebchen*," she called out, gesturing over my head, "you have to meet my little Stephanie – we were practically in kindergarten together."

I gave Nick the glare that I wanted to shove down her throat. This was all fun to him – he sent back a prim little smirk.

The other woman got up from their table and came over unhurriedly. "Hello," she said quietly, to each of us in turn.

"Dagmar – Stephanie. Isn't she fabulous? And this dreamboat accessory is her brother – what was it?"

Nick smiled up at Dagmar. "Nicholas Olsen. Nick."

Dagmar was tall and calm, with large, beautiful hands. Her expression was one of unflappable neutral amusement. She held out her hand and when he rose to take it she didn't step back. Their faces were inches from each other. You could sense the world of that restaurant, the voices, the music, dissolving around them. But he knew I was watching, all the same.

So was Angela. There was no mistaking that look, and no putting words to it. She traded my shoulder for Dagmar's and broke the spell. Nick sat down again, and crossed his eyes for my benefit. Angela loomed. "Dagmar's the brains in our stable," she said, and the big boys back at their table made suitable noises. "Our next big project, and, my darlings, it *is* big, is the Dagmeister's *solo bambino*."

The Dagmeister swished back her shoulder-length hair. "Just one of the team," she said. Her low, even voice matched her looks. She produced a card and handed it to Nick. "And what do you do?"

"I'm a gardener," he told her, looking straight back into her eyes. She wasn't meant to believe him.

"Cards, everyone," Angela demanded. I don't have a card.

"Well, you call me the next time you visit," she told me. "Lunch and catch up and topics unfathomable to man. But now we have to finish our meals, and get back to *der kommandoposten*." Dagmar didn't hasten to follow. She turned back to Nick.

"I might need a gardener. Call me next time you're in town."

"I live in town," he said, and gave her his card.

She scanned it and laughed. "Well, call me anyway." He watched her go back to their table. I stuck out my tongue at him. Smug brat, after all these years.

But Angela was Queen Bee, all right. Both queen and jester setting the table at a roar. The big boys anyway. They'd come in just after us and the tone of the bistro had changed at once. The waiters loved it; you could tell they knew all the routines. The rest of us were the audience. And truly, she was quick and funny and original; they were all, in their own way, smart, to be fair. Nick and I eavesdropped through dessert.

"She's a piece of work," I said, "but I guess she always was." And I looked at my smart, winsome, confident brother and started to laugh. He knows when his siblings are cutting him down to size – it's family language that goes way back. "What is it now?" he said, with mock resignation.

"That time in the stable, remember? Of course you do."

"I don't know what you're talking about."

"Oh, come on, Nikita, don't bullshit me. You and Boobsy, milking the cow." Do grown women giggle? Oh, yes. It was taking over. "Jesus, Nicky, it put me off drinking milk for years!"

He looked very solemn, which of course really got me going.

"You remember, alright. I bet you still fondle the memory."

A flush crept into his cheeks. "You know, Steph," he said, "you've always had this trivial side to your nature. That and your writer's compulsion to rake over the past."

"You're getting pompous, Nicky," I said.

"I've sometimes wondered," he ploughed on with his mean little speech, "whether that was why Jerry left you."

"Oh, really," I snapped. *And just why did Tricia leave you?* Well, I didn't actually say that, though he may have seen it in my eyes (which everyone says are identical to his).

"Sorry," he said, and meant it.

Nicky's a sweet man, a way better person than me, and I hadn't seen him for almost two years. But since we'd started lunch laughing about family skeletons – Cousin Janet's "little sister," and our grandfather "born an orphan" – his reaction seemed pretty ironic. I let it go, and leaned back to enjoy the last of the bright Sancerre that he'd chosen for us.

Dagmar, I realized, had been watching the family spat. I stared her down. Well, she looked away, anyway. Or maybe she was just getting her purse. The carnival was over.

Angela swooped across: "The meal's taken care of, children." Her stage whisper drawing all eyes.

Nick cut off my protests. "You're very kind," he said, and as she sailed off he grinned at me. "She does not brook contradiction," he whispered. It was a tag from our childhood – Uncle Raymond's wry catchphrase for Aunt Leonie.

The boys hovered at the door, kibitzing with the maître d', waiting their cue.

Dagmar's hand gave the slightest wave.

And Angela, framed by her courtiers, flashed gaiety at us all and then flexed her hands towards Nick and me in that pianist routine.

If I saw claws, I'd only myself to blame.

Nick gestured to our waiter. "Since lunch was free," he said, "I shall buy us a very good cognac." There's always something about Nick's ease in his world that makes me feel like a peasant.

When the drinks came, he raised his glass towards me. "Here's to the Queen Bee."

"She's a monster," I said.

"People who make it on their own can be like that," he said. "Think where she came from."

II

I wonder if they're still there, those scratches in the kitchen door-frame where Uncle Raymond measured our heights. After twenty-five years, I can conjure the smell of Tideswell so easily. I can almost put out my hand and feel the stable's brick wall, hot in the Ontario sun, for it was in August that we went there for, I don't know, maybe five years in a row.

It's as much a dream as a memory – the blue haze across the faces of the woodlots, which seemed like islands to me or like crouched wild animals among the cornfields and dairy herds. The high wooden barns with their stone foundations and the round silo towers at one end were so like the pictures of old European churches. I could imagine, from my bedroom's dormer window that I was in England or France in the time of St. Joan with visions, armies, and everywhere people on horses.

The farmhouses too, in red or yellow brick, so many aban-doned. There was one half a mile down the concession road with a jungle of day lilies in front, venomous at midday with deer flies that followed you like heat-seeking missiles. The ghosts of the long-gone family thickened the air there, somehow, past the broken doorway – the traces of wallpaper, mildewed books, even a child's rag doll that I adopted for a summer, though I never took her into the house or let anyone else know about her, of course. It was her previous owner I was drawn to. I was not a doll person, but ghosts were my passion and desire.

We were a shifting tribe – sharing some things together, but each wandering off on their own. By the last summer my older brother Keith had his own interests and a friend in the village who was home from university. Nicky's mark on the doorframe had climbed above mine at last, but we were confidants still, friends to the end.

Mom and her sisters shared a kind of despairing loyalty for Uncle Raymond. From childhood, I understood him to be "disappointed," and I expect he was in more ways than one, but it was really his marriage that they meant. Aunt Leonie was "Garbo" to them, and they didn't mean it kindly. "The Ice Queen," my mother called her once, when they'd been for a visit. "She thinks her pee's bloody Dom Perignon."

The mystery was why they'd ever got married. They had no children, and his legal practice in St Mary's was a part-time joke. The money all came from Aunt Leonie's side – she had a faint South African accent and I always imagined diamond and gold fields, never thinking in those days of the slaves who'd have toiled in those mines.

Their house was beautiful – seven miles out of the town, with a paddock and stable and open farmland all around. When you saw them out riding together across the back field, she on her dappled Arabian mare, and he on the old hunter, Michelangelo, you could imagine what brought them together. But together they weren't, in any other way.

Keith called Uncle Raymond "sheepish." He despised the air of conspiracy, the rueful shrugs and winks behind Aunt Leonie's back when she'd "laid down the law."

My uncle was a nice man, though, kind and gentle, with a pride in his appearance. He always wore ascots fluffed up at the neck, "cravats" as he called them, in muted colours. Once, he came upon me, off brooding on the steps by their lily pond. "Never mind, Trooper," he said, he always called me that and I loved it, though Aunt Leonie would shoot him a glance if he used it in company. He came down and sat next to me on the steps, and took my hand.

"When I feel blue," he said, almost as though he were talking to himself, "I take Michelangelo out by the river and pretend I'm in a faraway land, in a faraway time, and it all seems to come right." He put his arm round my shoulders. "Growing up's tricky, I know," he murmured. "And being grown-up's no hell either, Trooper."

That was in our last summer there. In fact, it's the only one of those summers that I truly remember – the swallows flashing over us to their nest in the stable, the clean smell of soap, and the comfort of feeling an equal. Then the broken spell when Aunt Leonie called down to us from an upstairs window, the intrusion we felt.

But I was drawn to Aunt Leonie, despite what everyone said. I think she was the disappointed one, really. Just too proud or too lonely to share it. Alone with her I felt the guilty pleasure of consorting with the enemy. She'd say, "Stevie and I need some time together," and at first unwillingly, but soon only waiting to be asked, I'd follow her up to her bedroom. I came to love being there, despite all the femininity, for the taste and stillness and the smell of that room. Without being forced, I was preparing, I think, to leave childhood behind.

She'd sit me in front of the window and brush my short hair with slow, trance-inducing strokes, while I stared at the medieval farmlands. She spoke to me about her girlhood in Stellenbosch and the things she felt counted in life. "Beauty," she said, "is our saviour. It puts us in harmony with ourselves, in a world of discord." A quaint way to talk to a fifteen-year-old girl. If I tried that on with my daughter we'd both be in stitches. But there was nothing quaint about Aunt Leonie – she was cool and elegant and firm. That room was her harmony, and she let me be part of it. There's something in children that will understand adults, intuit their worlds, if they know they have choice in the matter.

My uncle and aunt weren't the only mismatched couple in that township. Mr. Beaupré who delivered the eggs and cream had married a local girl and taken over her family's big, run-down farm. According to Keith's friend, Geordie, Mrs. Beaupré had been the local slut, several months pregnant by who knows whom, when this Frenchman turned up and married her and got nothing but contempt for doing so. They'd just the one daughter, and though Don Beaupré worked like a slave to get the farm back on its feet, they drank and fought and lived, Geordie said, in a pigsty.

Angie Beaupré was a few months older than me, and had no problems with her womanhood. Her tight sweaters and T-shirts flaunted her breasts when I was doing my best to conceal my own. She'd come up sometimes in the van with her father and hang around afterward by the stable. Uncle Raymond called her the Comanche. He said she rode better bareback than most men could in a saddle. She was slovenly and crude, but he let her ride Michelangelo two times a week and she'd urge the old thoroughbred into a gallop the moment she was mounted. Her hair flew back, her mouth was an ecstatic "O." "If that girl weren't so well built," he said, "she'd make a champion jockey. She's utterly fearless." It was Keith who first called her Boobsy.

I found her disgusting in most ways. She smelled so unwashed, so fleshly, and dragged sex into everything with a coarse, knowing snigger. But she knew the whole township by heart, and we sometimes went exploring and picnicking, the three of us. She read books too; she went up to the bookmobile every week and came back with an armful. She'd tell us their stories, often for an hour at a time, sitting on the riverbank or on the knoll above the old mill, but it was always the romance and "the juicy bits" that she dwelt on. She must have made some of them up too – I'm pretty sure there's no screwing in *Lorna Doone*, though I've never read it. She loved making me blush.

We went down to their farm to see the new puppies. They were in a corner of the ramshackle barn where they stalled their one cow at night. The collie bitch, all ribs and clotted hair, came whimpering out, her swollen teats brushing the floor. What's the pull towards baby animals, anyway? Even people who can't stand babies seem to feel it. Nicky and I were each cradling a puppy, just out of the blind stage, when Angie told us the father was Jimbo, Uncle Raymond's chocolate lab. "I caught them doing it by the front gate," she said, and then she got down on her knees and held the poor collie and mimed a whole vigorous fucking routine for us. "Then they caught the knot," she said, and let the bitch go back to her corner. "They was stuck for ten minutes, bum to bum, with these stupid looks on their faces, till his long pink worm of a thing came out all a-dangle."

Jimbo was my friend. He'd come and lay his head in my lap, looking at me with his brown soulful eyes. I felt sick imagining it, and she was laughing up in my face. Nicky was laughing too. "People do it that way too," she said. "I bet your mom and dad do. I've seen mine at it."

She could beat either one of us every time at the staring game.

Then there was the condom. She fished it out with a stick from under a bush. "You know what that's for, don't you?" she said. "Here, smell it." And she thrust it at my face so that I stumbled back and fell on the grass. She stood over me, laughing, with that white flaccid thing drooping over the stick, and its milky bulb. "Nicky knows what that smells like, doesn't he?" she sniggered, and then chased him with it, laughing down the lane.

We came back from a walk once and went to the barn again. Her father was in town and she had to do the milking that evening. The old Ayrshire cow came rambling in with us, and stood mumbling on a capful of oats while Boobsy set down the pail. "Here, I'll show you how," she said, and told Nicky to squat down beside her. I sat on the straw, watching under the cow's belly. She took one of the big teats and wagged it towards me. It felt vaguely obscene, but I wasn't aware back then how like an uncircumcised penis a cow's teat looks.

"You get hold of it close to the bag," she said, "and then squeeze around it, like this, see, and pull down, closing your fingers." The milk hissed into the pail. Laughing, she squirted a stream of it straight at my face. I was three feet away, but some of it ran down my cheek. I put out my tongue and tasted it, hot as blood. She took Nicky's hand and placed it on the next teat, and after a while he was getting the milk to come too. I was just going to ask for a turn at it, when I saw that her hand was on Nicky's thigh, sliding up the leg of his shorts. I couldn't see his face, I couldn't see hers either, but I stared in disbelief as she eased out his penis, big as I'd never imagined it, the skin drawn back over the purplish glans, and her fingers moving in the same rhythm as her other hand worked on the teat.

When he came, thin drops spurting out onto the ground, I let out a wail of disgust and fled out of the barn. I could hear her deep laughter triumphant behind me.

We never mentioned it, ever. That summer was the last of many things.

Aunt Leonie left in the winter. She just took off. The house was sold, and nobody heard from her again.

Except that when I was nineteen and came home from Art School for my birthday, there was a package waiting, with giraffe and cheetah stamps on it. It was a skirt and blouse, in soft, full-bodied cottons, cream and magnolia, with the palest grey silk scarf to match. There was a card with a pen-and-wash drawing of a gazelle, drinking from its reflection in a pool. I have it still. Inside are nine words in her sloping, precise hand: *Stevie dear. Don't give yourself away. With love, Leonie.* There was no return address.

I hung the outfit in the closet at home. It was beautiful, but way too *soigné* for the person I thought I was then.

But a year later I tried it on before the Graduation Ball. How did she know what would fit me?

That was the night I met Andrew. The night I first kissed him, rest his soul.

III

There's no point in saying I shouldn't have gone. I went.

At the time, it didn't feel like I had much choice.

She phoned me at Nick's the evening I got back to the city. We were out on the balcony, having our first drink, and I couldn't make out her words above the traffic noise. I took the phone inside.

"Lunch tomorrow, Stephie. Tallulah's, you'll love it, *muy simpático*, we must talk."

Stephie.

"How did you know I was here?" I asked.

"From Dagmar, sweetie – you're out of the loop. But listen, lunch tomorrow. I know all about you, and I've got work for you, good work. It's serious money, darling, up front if you need it, and believe me you could do it in your sleep."

The sum she whispered was thirty times my last royalty cheque.

I was broke, Leni's teeth needed fixing, what could I say?
She'd pick me up at 11:00.

"So," I said as I handed the phone back to Nick. "Dagmar? Quick work, Casanova." I'd only been gone a week.

"She's wonderful, Steph."

I know the signs. I've looked into my own eyes in the glass, and wondered at myself, shaken and thrilled to be in that place again. We're love junkies, both of us, Nick and I. Keith is the only one who really grew up. (I suppose I should envy him and his dear, sensible family but where would that get me?)

"Okay," I said, "I'm glad for you, Nicky. And so maybe you know what all this is about? Before you start in on the raptures."

"Yes, I do," he said, as his boyish, confiding eyes refocused themselves. "And this is the tricky thing, Steph. Angela wants you to work on a couple of scripts – no, listen, she's serious; she's been reading your work."

"Then she must be deluded," I said. "But anyway, what?"

"Well, you see, Dagmar's starting her own company."

I wasn't following this, and I said so.

"Well, she has to sort out her legal position before she leaves."

"Why?"

"Well, the white slave project is in her name, but Soft Touch might think they have a claim on it."

"Nick," I said, "I'm slow on the uptake sometimes, but you seem to find the street more interesting than me, and your every answer has begun with 'Well.' You're hiding something, little brother."

He laughed and turned to face me. "And you're getting rusty, Steph. I'm not that transparent." This was the fourth Nick I'd seen in less than an hour – assured, rather dominating in fact. His business face, I presumed. He leaned back on the railing. "Dagmar wants you to know that she can offer you work, so you needn't rush into Angela's arms. Just keep it to yourself for now, okay?"

"They're both nuts," I said. "What the hell do I know about TV?"

He took my glass. "TV's got to change," he said. "Let's go inside."

We drank Prosecco, the happy drink, while he made crepes and a rocket tangerine salad. Where did he learn his ways? He's the aristocrat among us – equally at ease in a greasy spoon or at the Savoy or, I saw now, in his own nifty kitchen with his French skillets and German knives. For me, this felt like slumming in reverse, but I'm used to that. My family doesn't rub it in – in some ways they choose to admire me.

There was a woman's toiletry bag in the bathroom, a lavender peignoir hanging on the door. I fell asleep in the spare room, on a bed worth a thousand bucks, thinking of money.

Next day the intercom buzzed at 11:30. I went down to see Angela waving me over from a car window across the street. She was talking on her cellphone, but snapped it shut as I slid into the back. "You look fantastic," she said, turning in her seat. "You look disgustingly young."

The car pulled out and then braked, with a screech. I was jolted almost into her face and saw the fear in her eyes replaced by a fury that she turned on the driver. He pointed to a car changing lanes ahead of us, and the moment was over. She laughed, and turned back towards me: "Just another DWO."

"DWO?"

"Driving While Oriental, dear heart. Signal right, turn left, *BOK GWAI KUI TAO!*"

A block further on, the driver's cellphone rang. "Speak to me," he said, and then, "Hi Solly, I'm on my way."

Angela leaned towards him: "Tell him they're either in or they're out. If he doesn't like it he can screw himself."

The driver smirked into the phone: "You heard that, I suppose?" His eyes flicked up to mine in the rearview mirror –

detached like that they looked weak and ruthless. "I'll be there in ten," he said, and pocketed his phone.

Angela skimmed her fingers along the seat back. "Finagling bastard," she muttered.

"Dog eat dog world?" I murmured.

She let out a short laugh. "In this 'hood, sweetie, it's bitch eat dog, every time." She patted the driver's shoulder. "Marvin here's our contract lawyer. We pay him spectacularly. Meet Stephanie, doll – she's coming on board."

Marvin winked at me in the mirror.

Then her phone rang.

"Yes, Chicken," she said, "what's popping?

"Well, of course you do.

"He can be a doofus, can't he? Is he there? Give him the phone."

The car came to a stop and she gestured that we should get out. "This is just a time waste," she was saying. "If she needs it, let her get it."

She got out of the car, aimed a quick finger-pistol at Marvin and marched on ahead of me. The same good suit, but in purply brown with shoes that would pay my month's rent. My jeans and cotton sweater made their own statement; I'd thought about it. I caught up with her. "Just give her the goddamn Bay card, okay?" She snapped her phone shut, and turned at the restaurant door. "Daughter, seventeen. Mad for clothes." We went in.

Tallulah's was pretty transgendered. Art deco with *très* campy accessories. It was like the dining hall of a small luxury liner (as if I've ever been on one) made over by Divine. The early lunchers who'd half-filled the place seemed to come from both camps. They all seemed like regulars. And so, evidently, was she.

Her flamboyance appalled me. She sashayed toward a table across the room, and I cringed in her wake. I had to meet Basil ("Antonia's agent and a very wicked creature") and "dear Peter" who was in casting. The eager young couple who shared their table didn't count, apparently. I was a *guionista macanuda* (which had a ring to it; I looked it up later) as well as being manna from heaven, her childhood sweetheart, and a very dark horse, all in one wraparound sentence. The three modish women at the next table were drinking it up. Basil was maybe fifty, with unhealthy cheeks and combed-across hair. Of all the looks a man can give you, that slimy prejudgement is maybe the worst. I hope my eyes put a chill through his liver, but I doubt it.

Angela was waving to someone at the bar. "Now," she said, "you get to meet Adam Chow and his latest catamite."

"That's enough of this," I hissed. No, I didn't hiss – I ground it out through my teeth. "I won't do this."

Her eyes flicked to mine. I was ready to walk out but she took my arm without missing a gay beat. "But first we have plots to hatch, angel hearts, and contracts to sign. *Ciao ciao, banditti.*" Dear Peter giggled, the young couple beamed, the Basil stared pointedly at my crotch. When a svelte young waiter appeared at our side, she took his arm too and practically waltzed us to our table. There was an ice bucket and wine, which the boy uncorked with a flourish as we sat down. I might as well not have been there for him; his eyes were fixed upon her as he filled our glasses. Does everyone in Toronto drink Prosecco in July?

The pillar behind her had a mirror inset, and I shifted my chair to put her between me and my own face. I could see half the room reflected, though, and faces at two or three tables all staring our way. At least that's how it felt.

She raised her glass to me, and halfway through drinking gave a Greek finger-wave to someone behind me.

I took a sip. The bubbles tickled my lips. She was waving at someone else now.

"You seem to know everyone." I said.

"I probably do," she said. "And I can whip all their asses at pool." Her glass was half empty already. Maybe she drank them under the table too.

The waiter hovered. She stopped him before he could hand us the menus.

"We're having the tornedos," she told him, and patted his wrist: "*Sonrosados, chico.*" And to me: "Trust me, you'll love it." I almost said I was vegetarian, but it was more fun to watch the boy make dove's eyes at her, and peek at himself in the glass pillar before his little hips snaked off with him back to the kitchen.

"Just give me a minute, sweetie, while I clear the decks." Angela was intent on her cellphone, her thumb agile on the keys. Downturned like that, her face had a jowly heaviness, and her carefully powdered nose couldn't hide its wide pores, but I could envy the luxury of that hair – the dark wave upon wave that matched her own energy. She'd unbuttoned her jacket, and the blouse was a cotton so fine and white that you wanted to reach out and touch it.

Then I realized she was looking at me – an unnerving, calculating gaze. And her eyes were deep violet, which I hadn't noticed or remembered. Coloured lenses, maybe. I felt caught out, somehow, and took a good drink from my wine.

"Okay," she said, and put the cellphone away. "I've turned it off. No more distractions."

Her hand, with its rings and carmine nails, swooped up the bottle and came to refill my glass.

"Turkey talk, girlfriend. Let's get to it."

The bubbles rose in little chains to the surface.

I met her eyes again. "Well?"

"You get by, Stephanie, don't you? As a writer."

"Yes," I said, "I get by."

"Well, I'm a realist," she said. "I've read your work, and you don't belong in a world where you just fucking get by."

"Oh, really," I said, and I was about to explain that I didn't belong in a world of darlings and sweeties and Basils and dog-eating bitches and gigolo waiters and expense-account lunches either. But she cut me off with a "Shush now." I was ready to hit her.

"You can help us, we can help you; it's as simple as that." She spoke in a lower pitch, eyes fixed upon mine. The frivolity had vanished. "We have to bring these girls to life, and quickly. You've got the goods. That's why the offer's so generous."

I couldn't keep up. "What girls?" I asked. "What are you talking about?"

"I just got the scripts back from someone I trust, and what did he say? That we'd got the main characters wrong. And he was dead right."

She talked rapidly, emphatically, pressing her fingers on the tablecloth.

"It's got to be the girls' story as much as the headliners'. Right now they're just bimbos, victims, nothings. We've really screwed up."

My glass was almost empty. Something was dawning on me, and I didn't like it one bit.

"I need stories for these girls," she said, and leaned back in her chair, her hands behind her head. Her blouse gaped between two of the buttons, and a crease of skin showed through, yellowish against the white cotton. "We need stories, subplots that run through two or three episodes. That's where you earn your money."

"Just a minute," I said, but she wasn't giving me air. She leaned forward again. "No, listen. We've got a Romanian girl, a Latvian, a Filipina. They could all have good stories. Back story, front story, anything you can dream up to bring them to life. We need characters, not props."

"I'll think about it," I said.

"No time for thinking, sweetie. We present to HBO at the end of the month; we're under the *cannone grande*."

So that was it. I'd never forgive Nick for this.

"You're talking about the white slavery thing, aren't you?"

"Well, what did you think?"

"I *thought* – that was Dagmar's *solo bambino*."

It was hard to describe the look she gave me. I wouldn't have called it amused.

"I've taken over the Creative on this one," she said. "Dagmar's working on contract stuff this week."

Yes, I thought, but didn't say, *I just bet she is.*

Angela watched me for two beats, narrowing her eyes. "Come on," she said, "I give you the basics, you give me faces, stories, families, whatever. For you that comes naturally. Have fun with it, Stephanie – free rein, *carte blanche, assoluto*."

"No," I said, "I don't think I can do this." I was fiddling with my glass, wondering how to escape. Whatever I did, I was compromised.

She reached for the bottle and filled me up again, talking as she did so: "*An eerie ability to enter the minds and voices of the dispossessed*" and "*dramatic moments that reveal intelligence and sensitivity where you'd least expect to find them*."

I laughed, more to appease my flattery radar than anything else. Her memory was impressive but, "No," I repeated. "Reviews and cover blurbs don't tell you anything."

There was a hand on my shoulder, and a rich, ragged voice said, "Angela darling, you mustn't forget me, you know." A thin, pretty woman, about my own age, was leaning on me. She smelled of cloves and cigarette smoke.

"Sweetheart! I thought you were in Montreal. You look just fantastic!" Angela's voice climbed an octave; it was performance-on-demand. "You must talk to dear Peter – there's all kinds of filming in town, seven features, perfect timing for you." Her sparkle and gladness was beaming across the table; I'd a ringside view. "Let's get you back to work, treasure – tune you up again, and we'll talk in the fall. I've a thousand ideas."

"I've left two messages, Angie."

"I know, I know, but we're in stark crazy loony *scatenati* mode – ask Stephie here – deadlines looming, backers finking out on us, scriptwriters jumping off bridges."

The woman's fingertips pressed on my collar bone. "I need to see you," she said. In the pillar glass her eyes were huge and troubled, the fine cheekbones too close to the surface. I knew her from somewhere.

"September, hon, September," Angela crooned. "All this crapola will be history by then. Make sure to call me. Tell Carla I said it's priority – we'll do dinner and really talk prospects. Now you go and catch Peter before he leaves." And she turned back to me.

I heard a small, moaning noise. "Oh, fuck yourself," the woman said, and stalked off.

Angela's eyes were fierce for a moment. Then "Jesus wept," she said, and slowly exhaled.

"But I know her," I said. "I saw her at Stratford in *Miss Julie*. Yes, Sheila Ricard. It is, isn't it? She was brilliant."

"And how long ago was that?" Angela took a bread roll from the wicker basket and then put it back again. She leaned her elbows on the table. "Whatever talent she had disappeared up her nose long ago," she said. "Let's not lose our thread here, sweetie. Just sketch out some stories for us, if that's all you've got time for. I'll get someone to take it from there."

And it's funny, ridiculous really, but I bristled at that. I'd no intention now of taking the job. I was furious with Nick, yet wondering too if he might not have known, if Dagmar was maybe using us both. I hated having this secret I couldn't reveal; and I was spooked by that scene with Sheila Ricard, by the rage and defeat that still clung to me with her scent. But at the same time (how can our brains do so much in one moment?) I already had my Latvian girl – my gambler with her faith in her guardian angel despite all the blows, and the secret part of her no one could ever betray, and the promises she'd made to herself early on and would keep. She was precious and wretched – and the thought that some hack scriptwriter might saddle her with his clichés was an outrage.

I laughed and drank some more wine.

"I don't know why you would think I could do this," I said.

"I'm good at what *I* do, Stephanie. I do my work; I don't fake things. I've read everything you've published and I want you in."

Yeah, right, I thought, and didn't say. I didn't need to.

"Want to try me?"

What a shape-shifter she was. Suddenly this was a person who maybe did more with her kids than shove credit cards in their hands. Her face was alight with fun. She wanted to play.

And for a moment there, we were back in the old staring game. This was a different Boobsy, though, one I'd forgotten or perhaps had never acknowledged. No leer, no snigger. Just a girl who wanted to play.

"Go on," she said. "Try me." And just as in the old days, she won. I looked away, and saw myself in the mirror, smiling.

"Okay," I said. "Okay. There's my story called *While You Were Sleeping.*"

"Your last book," she said.

"I've only done two."

She ignored that. "I read it last night. The second wife reading the dead wife's diaries."

"Okay, you win. And so?"

"Come on, try me again."

It was kind of infectious. Maybe the Prosecco was helping. I said there was a story that had a fox and a carpenter in it (I couldn't remember the title myself for some reason).

"And the shy French trapper woman who left rabbits for him on his porch. I really liked that one," she said. "I recognized the place too. It was Trugg's Bridge, wasn't it, down by the mill?"

That wasn't the bridge I'd had in my mind's eye at all; I'd just made one up. But then, we all set the things that we read in places we know, from life or from movies – that's why so much descriptive writing's a waste of time.

But she really had read it. It's nice to be read.

"I wish this was just a social visit," I said. "Meeting you last week brought a lot of things back I'd forgotten."

She gave a faint smile. "Well, I live in the present, lovey; it's quite busy enough. *Temps perdu, et pas de récherche, ma chèrie.*"

Some instinct in me was at work. "I don't know how you got to be where you are, Angela, but I remember you telling us stories, Nicky and me, up above that old mill. All those books that you'd read."

She looked almost alarmed, and drew her elbows back off the table. "That's a good way to be remembered," she said. "But—"

"And your riding," I said. I could see how uneasy she was, wanting to get back to business, but I felt in control, and I was trying to like her. "You were amazing, you know. I hadn't realized till now how much I envied you." As I said it, I knew it was true, and I just kept on talking.

"But you were bad, you know. You loved making me squirm, didn't you? I was such an innocent."

I couldn't stop myself.

"You were the girl who jerked off my brother in the barn while I was watching."

It was as if we were in an echo chamber, the sounds of the other diners, remote all at once. My laughter harsh and empty.

She was staring at me with something that looked like contempt. Her lips twisted for a moment to one side, and then she leaned forward.

"Listen, sweetie," she said, and I knew in that instant, before the words left her lips, what was coming; and I saw in her eyes – and this also before her words were out – not pain or sorrow so much as a kind of triumph.

"Listen, sweetie," it came, "you don't want to know where I learned to do that."

"Okay," I said, and swirled my wine glass in both hands, looking at the light fixture mirrored there, swaying on the surface.

She'd meant it as a depth charge, the lost piece of a long-ago jigsaw puzzle, picked up in the musty corner of the stable where it had lain, sheepish and unsuspected, for twenty years.

I hooked my arm over my chair back and looked around me. It *was* like a liner, a ship of fools, a charade. *The hell with it,* I was thinking. *We're all damaged goods one way or another.*

I finished my wine and turned back to face her.

"I still think it's funny," I said.

She didn't realize, for a moment, that I'd got it. Her eyes flared and then, when she saw, they went blank at me. She dashed her palm, with a funny childlike grimace, across her mouth and reached down for her purse. The dark waves of hair were all I could see of her. She started rummaging on her lap for something that I'm half sure wasn't there.

I felt the tug of shame and pity. How could I be such a bitch? Knowing what I knew too.

She came up with her cellphone and looked out across the room as she dialed. With her face uplifted, her jawline was strong and defined – no hint of the jowls now, a handsome, confident woman. "Carlotta," she said "I'll need those scripts in an hour – I'll call when we're close and you can bring them down to the cab. *Si, si, molto gradevole. Ciao, Adorata.*"

I don't know what she'd have done next, or what I might have said, but that's when the food arrived. "Pablito, Pablito," she sang to the waiter, and as he set down our plates, she ran her hand up and down his ribs. "Isn't he just too exquisite for words?" Pablito danced off for the pepper mill, and when he came back she kept stroking him as he performed. "Waste, waste," she said to the world at large. "All those juicy young girls with nothing to hope for." I heard laughter from a table behind me, somebody whistled, and the boy bowed adoringly to her and went on his way.

Our plates were like two still lifes on the table between us.

Angela picked up her glass, which was still half full, and tilted it towards me. "Come on, now," she said. "You need the money. Let's talk while we eat."

The last two minutes might never have happened.

You brave, awful woman, I thought, and I couldn't stand it. "Listen," I said, and reached over and touched her wrist. "I've had it with secrets. There's something you ought to know."

But she spoke instead, quietly, almost without expression, setting her glass down and flexing her fingers. "Dagmar has screwed herself," she said. "And by this time tomorrow she'll know it."

She picked up her fork. "So, let's get started, before these tornedos get frostbite. You know you can do it. Which girl do you think we can find the best story line for?"

My Swiss sister-in-law used to tell their children about Sprugli and Sprigli. They live in your little fingers, and they change places when the sun goes behind the clouds. Sprigli's voice is like honey, and whispers bad thoughts in your ear. Sprugli's voice is like salt, and tells you the truth.

I counted to three.

"Isn't Dagmar a Latvian name?"

She let out a small, barking "Ha," then flourished her fork and speared a green bean. She held it up between us, turning it slowly back and forth. And there was Boobsy again, the one I'd been blind to, with her violet eyes teasing, ready to play.

"I think it's more Danish," she said, "but let's go with it anyway."

Halli Villegas of Mount Forest, Ontario, is the author of three collections of poetry (*Red Promises, In the Silence Absence Makes,* and *The Human Cannonball*)and a collection of ghost stories, *The Hairwreath and Other Stories.* She received Honourable Mention for two of her stories in the 2010 edition of The Year's Best Horror edited by Ellen Datlow. She is the co-editor of the anthologies *Imaginarium: The Best Canadian Speculative Writing 2012* and *In the Dark: Tales of the Supernatural.* Her genre work has appeared in anthologies that include *Chilling Tales 2, The White Collar Anthology, Bad Seed, Incubus, Girls Who Bite Back* and *Mammoth Best New Horror, 25th anniversary edition.*

(photo: Liz Westbrook-Trenholm)

Seán Virgo lives in southwest Saskatchewan. He was born in Malta and raised in several countries, and became a Canadian at the age of 32. Since then his short fiction and poetry have been anthologized and won awards on both sides of the Atlantic, including National Magazine Awards in both genres, and the CBC and BBC3 competitions for short fiction. His work has been translated into numerous European languages, and Farsi. He has published one novel, *Selakhi* (Exile Editions), and over the years has worked in theatre and mixed-media as writer, director and performer, as well as writing and hosting the TV series *Middle of Somewhere*. He founded the literary magazine *TickleAce* in Newfoundland, and created *Requiem*, a stage performance with a youthful Haida cast, as a challenging presentation to the Department of Indian Affairs. His most recent fiction collection is *Dibidalen, ten stories.*

Iryn Tushabe is originally from Uganda, and is a writer and independent journalist now living in Saskatchewan. Her creative non-fiction has appeared in *Briarpatch Magazine* and her literary journalism in *Prairies North Magazine*. She's at work on a first novel. (photo: Maureen Mugerw)

Katherine Fawcett of Squamish, British Columbia, has published the short story collection *The Little Washer of Sorrows*, which was shortlisted for a Sunburst Award for Excellence in Canadian Fiction of the Fantastical. Her writing has also been featured in *Geist, Event Magazine, subTerrain* and *FreeFall*. She is currently working on a second short story collection.   katherinefawcett.com   (photo: Anastasia Chomlack)

Darlene Madott of Toronto is a family-law lawyer and award-winning writer of seven books. She has twice won the Bressani Literary Award, once for the title story of *Making Olives and Other Family Secrets*, and for her collection *Stations of the Heart* (Exile Editions). This is the second time her fiction has been short-listed for the Carter V. Cooper award.   darlenemadott.com   (photo: Mark Tearle)

Jane Callen of Victoria, British Columbia, has been awarded the Elizabeth Krehm Mentorship from Ryerson University, a year after winning their 2013 Chang Prize in Short Fiction. She was a finalist in *Malahat Review*'s Open Season Awards (Fiction, 2014), and is a creative writing graduate from Humber University. She has completed a novel, drafted a second, and is working on a collection of short stories.

Yakos Spilotouplos of Toronto has published short stories in journals including *ELQ/Exile* magazine and *The Nashwaak Review*, and in the collection *Everything Change: An Anthology of Climate Fiction*. His work has been shortlisted for several awards, including the Carter V. Cooper Short Fiction Competition (CVC3, and now CVC7), the 2016 Writers Union of Canada Short Prose Competition, and the 2016 Climate Fiction Short Story Contest held by Arizona State University. He has completed a novel and is hard at work on a second.

Chris Urquhart of Toronto has has appeared in *Adbusters, COLORS Magazine, Maisonneuve, The Santiago Times* and *VICE*. She is a two-time Canada Council grant recipient, past SSHRC fellow, and Ontario Graduate Scholar. Her first non-fiction book, *Dirty Kids: Chasing Freedom with American Nomads,* was published in September 2017.

(photo : Alex Berceanu)

Norman Snider of Toronto is a screenwriter, author, journalist and professor. He has published *How to Make Love to a Movie Star* and *The Roaring Eighties and Other Good Times* (both with Exile Editions), *Smokescreen: One Man Against the Underworld,* and *The Changing of the Guard.* For film, he co-wrote – with David Cronenberg – *Dead Ringers,* and most recently *Casino Jack*, starring Kevin Spacey (also brought out as a book with Exile Editions).

Linda Rogers of Victoria, British Columbia, is a past Poet Laureate and Canadian People's Poet of Victoria who writes poetry, fiction, song lyrics, scripts, and literary criticism. She has been awarded the Gwendolyn MacEwen, Livesay, Leacock, National Poetry, Rukeyser, Acorn, Cardiff, Montreal, Kenney, Voices Israel, Prix Anglais and Bridport literary prizes. Recent titles include *Tempo Rubato,* and *Bozuk* (Exile Editions). Forthcoming is *Crow Jazz* and *Repairing the Hive*, fiction.

Carly Vandergriendt is a Montreal-based writer and translator. Her writing has appeared in *The Fiddlehead, Plenitude, Matrix, Room, Cosmonaut's Avenue, (parenthetical)* among others. A recent graduate of UBC's optional-residency MFA in Creative Writing, she is currently at work on her first novel. carlyrosalie.com @carlyrosalie

Exile's $15,000 Carter V. Cooper Short Fiction Competition

FOR CANADIAN WRITERS ONLY

$10,000 for the Best Story by an Emerging Writer
$5,000 for the Best Story by a Writer at Any Career Point

The shortlisted are published in the annual *CVC Short Fiction Anthology Series* and a selected group in *ELQ/Exile: The Literary Quarterly*

Exile's $3,000 Gwendolyn MacEwen Poetry Competition

FOR CANADIAN WRITERS ONLY

$1,500 for the Best Suite of Poetry
$1,000 for the Best Suite by an Emerging Writer
$500 for the Best Poem

Winners are published in *ELQ/Exile: The Literary Quarterly*

These annual competitions open in November
Details at: www.ExileQuarterly.com